Shauna &
S O Lee : Merry Xmas
From Santa 1975

"He went right on about his business."
FRONTISPIECE. *See page 68.*

BURGESS TRADE QUADDIES MARK

MOTHER WEST WIND "WHY" STORIES

BY

THORNTON W. BURGESS

Illustrations by
HARRISON CADY

GROSSET & DUNLAP

PUBLISHERS   NEW YORK

By arrangement with Little, Brown, and Company

PRINTED IN THE UNITED STATES OF AMERICA

CONTENTS

LIST OF ILLUSTRATIONS

I

WHY STRIPED CHIPMUNK IS PROUD OF HIS STRIPES

THE Merry Little Breezes of Old Mother West Wind are great friends of Striped Chipmunk. They hurry to call on him the very first thing every morning after Old Mother West Wind has brought them down from the Purple Hills. They always beg him to stop and play with them, but often he refuses. But he does it in such a merry way and with such a twinkle in his eyes that the Merry Little Breezes never get cross because he won't play. No, Sir, they never get cross. If anything, they think just a little bit more of Striped Chipmunk because he won't play. You see, they know that the reason he won't play is because he has work to do, and Striped Chipmunk believes and says:

"When there is work for me to do
The sooner started, sooner through."

So every morning they ask him to play, and every morning they laugh when he says he has too much to do. Then they rumple up his hair and pull his whiskers and give him last tag and race down to the Smiling Pool to see Grandfather Frog and beg him for a story. Now Grandfather Frog is very old and very wise, and he knows all about the days when the world was young. When he is feeling just right, he dearly loves to tell about those long-ago days.

One morning the Merry Little Breezes

found Grandfather Frog sitting as usual on his big green lily-pad, and they knew by the way he folded his hands across his white and yellow waistcoat that it was full of foolish green flies.

"Oh, Grandfather Frog, please do tell us why it is that Striped Chipmunk has such beautiful stripes on his coat," begged one of the Merry Little Breezes.

"Chug-a-rum! They are stripes of honor," replied Grandfather Frog, in his deep, gruff voice.

"Honor! Oh, how lovely! Do tell us about it! Please do!" begged the Merry Little Breezes.

"Chug-a-rum!" began Grandfather Frog, his big, goggly eyes twinkling. "Once upon a time, when the world was young, old Mr. Chipmunk, the grandfather a thousand times removed of Striped Chipmunk, lived very much as Striped Chipmunk does now. He was always very busy, very busy, indeed, and it was always about his own affairs. 'By attending strictly to my own business, I have no time to meddle with the affairs of my neighbors, and so I keep out of trouble,' said old Mr. Chipmunk."

"Just what Striped Chipmunk says now," broke in one of the Merry Little Breezes.

"That shows that he is just as wise as was his grandfather a thousand times removed, about whom I am telling you," replied Grandfather Frog. "Old Mr. Chipmunk wore just a little, plain brown coat. It didn't worry him a bit, not a bit, that his coat was just plain brown. It kept him just as warm as if it were a beautiful red, like that of Mr. Fox, or handsome black and white, like that of Mr. Skunk. He was perfectly satisfied with his little plain brown coat and took the best of care of it.

"One day as he was hurrying home to dinner, he climbed up on an old stump to look around and make sure that the way was clear. Over in a little path in the meadow grass was walking old Mr. Meadow Mouse. He was strolling along as if there was nothing in the world to fear. Way back behind him in the same little path, walking very fast but very quietly, was big Mr. Bob Cat. His eyes were yellow, and a hungry look was in them. He didn't see Mr. Meadow Mouse, but he would in a few minutes. Mr. Chipmunk saw that he would, and that there was no place for Mr. Meadow Mouse to hide.

" 'Humph! I never meddle in other people's affairs, and this is none of my business,' said little Mr. Chipmunk.

"But old Mr. Meadow Mouse was a friend. He thought a great deal of Mr. Meadow Mouse, did little Mr. Chipmunk. He couldn't bear to think of what would happen to Mr. Meadow Mouse if big Mr. Bob Cat should catch him. Then, almost without realizing what he was doing, little Mr. Chipmunk began to shout at big Mr. Bob Cat and to call him names. Of course big Mr. Bob Cat looked up right away and saw little Mr. Chipmunk sitting on the old stump. His eyes grew yellower and yellower, he drew his lips back from his long, sharp teeth in a very angry way, and his little bob tail twitched and twitched. Then, with great leaps, he came straight for the old stump on which little Mr. Chipmunk was sitting.

"Little Mr. Chipmunk didn't wait for him to get there. Oh, my, no! He took one good look at those fierce, hungry, yellow eyes and long, cruel teeth, and then he whisked into a hole in the old stump. You see, there wasn't time to go

anywhere else. Big Mr. Bob Cat found
the hole in the stump right away. He
snarled when he saw it. You see it was
too small, very much too small, for him
to get into himself. But he could get
one hand and arm in, and he did, feeling
all around inside for little Mr. Chipmunk.
Little Mr. Chipmunk was frightened
almost to death. Yes, Sir, he was frightened almost to death. He made himself
just as flat as he could on the bottom of
the hollow and held his breath.

"'You'd better come out of there,
Mr. Chipmunk, or I'll pull you out!'
snarled Mr. Bob Cat.

"Little Mr. Chipmunk just snuggled
down flatter than ever and didn't say a
word. Mr. Bob Cat felt round and round
inside the hollow stump and raked his
long claws on the sides until little Mr.
Chipmunk's hair fairly stood up. Yes.
Sir, it stood right up on end, he was so

scared. When it did that, it tickled the claws of Mr. Bob Cat. Mr. Bob Cat grinned. It was an ugly grin to see. Then he reached in a little farther and made a grab for little Mr. Chipmunk. His wide-spread, sharp claws caught in little Mr. Chipmunk's coat near the neck and tore little strips the whole length of it.

"Of course little Mr. Chipmunk squealed with pain, for those claws hurt dreadfully, but he was glad that his coat tore. If it hadn't, Mr. Bob Cat would surely have pulled him out. After a long time, Mr. Bob Cat gave up and went off, growling and snarling. When he thought it was safe, little Mr. Chipmunk crawled out of the old stump and hurried home. He ached and smarted terribly, and his little plain brown coat was torn in long strips.

" 'This is what I get for meddling in

the affairs of other folks!' said little Mr. Chipmunk bitterly. 'If I'd just minded my own business, it wouldn't have happened.'

"Just then he happened to look over to the house of Mr. Meadow Mouse. There was Mr. Meadow Mouse playing with his children. He didn't know a thing about what his neighbor, little Mr. Chipmunk, had done for him, for you remember he hadn't seen Mr. Bob Cat at all. Little Mr. Chipmunk grinned as well as he could for the pain.

" 'I'm glad I did it,' he muttered. 'Yes, Sir, I'm glad I did it, and I'm glad that Neighbor Meadow Mouse doesn't know about it. I'm glad that nobody knows about it.

'A kindly deed's most kindly done
    In secret wrought, and seen of none.

And so I'm glad that no one knows.'

"Now just imagine how surprised little

Mr. Chipmunk was, when in the fall it came time to put on a new coat, to have Old Mother Nature hand him out a beautiful striped coat instead of the little plain brown coat he had expected. Old Mother Nature's eyes twinkled as she said:

" 'There's a stripe for every tear made in your old coat by the claws of Mr. Bob Cat the day you saved Mr. Meadow Mouse. They are honor stripes, and hereafter you and your children and your children's children shall always wear stripes.'

"And that is how it happens that Striped Chipmunk comes by his striped coat, and why he is so proud of it, and takes such good care of it," concluded Grandfather Frog.

II

WHY PETER RABBIT CANNOT FOLD HIS HANDS

II

WHY PETER RABBIT CANNOT FOLD HIS HANDS

HAPPY JACK SQUIRREL sat with his hands folded across his white waistcoat. He is very fond of sitting with his hands folded that way. A little way from him sat Peter Rabbit. Peter was sitting up very straight, but his hands dropped right down in front. Happy Jack noticed it.

"Why don't you fold your hands the way I do, Peter Rabbit?" shouted Happy Jack.

"I — I — don't want to," stammered Peter.

"You mean you can't!" jeered Happy Jack.

Peter pretended not to hear, and a few minutes later he hopped away towards the dear Old Briar-patch, lipperty-lipperty-lip. Happy Jack watched him go, and there was a puzzled look in Happy Jack's eyes.

"I really believe he can't fold his hands," said Happy Jack to himself, but speaking aloud.

"He can't, and none of his family can," said a gruff voice.

Happy Jack turned to find Old Mr. Toad sitting in the Lone Little Path.

"Why not?" asked Happy Jack.

"Ask Grandfather Frog; he knows," replied Old Mr. Toad, and started on about his business.

And this is how it happens that Grandfather Frog told this story to the little meadow and forest people gathered around him on the bank of the Smiling Pool.

"Chug-a-rum!" said Grandfather Frog.
"Old Mr. Rabbit, the grandfather a
thousand times removed of Peter Rabbit,
was always getting into trouble. Yes,
Sir, old Mr. Rabbit was always getting
into trouble. Seemed like he wouldn't
be happy if he couldn't get into trouble.
It was all because he was so dreadfully
curious about other people's business, just
as Peter Rabbit is now. It seemed that
he was just born to be curious and so,
of course, to get into trouble.

"One day word came to the Green
Forest and to the Green Meadows that
Old Mother Nature was coming to see
how all the little meadow and forest
people were getting along, to settle all
the little troubles and fusses between
them, and to find out who were and who
were not obeying the orders she had
given them when she had visited them
last. My, my, my, such a hurrying and

scurrying and worrying as there was! You see, everybody wanted to look his best when Old Mother Nature arrived. Yes, Sir, everybody wanted to look his best.

"There was the greatest changing of clothes you ever did see. Old King Bear put on his blackest coat. Mr. Coon and Mr. Mink and Mr. Otter sat up half the night brushing their suits and making them look as fine and handsome as they could. Even Old Mr. Toad put on a new suit under his old one, and planned to pull the old one off and throw it away as soon as Old Mother Nature should arrive. Then everybody began to fix up their homes and make them as neat and nice as they knew how — everybody but Mr. Rabbit.

"Now Mr. Rabbit was lazy. He didn't like to work any more than Peter Rabbit does now. No, Sir, old Mr.

Rabbit was afraid of work. The very sight of work scared old Mr. Rabbit. You see, he was so busy minding other people's business that he didn't have time to attend to his own. So his brown and gray coat always was rumpled and tumbled and dirty. His house was a tumble-down affair in which no one but Mr. Rabbit would ever have thought of living, and his garden — oh, dear me, such a garden you never did see! It was all weeds and brambles. They filled up the yard, and old Mr. Rabbit actually couldn't have gotten into his own house if he hadn't cut a path through the brambles.

"Now when old Mr. Rabbit heard that Old Mother Nature was coming, his heart sank way, way down, for he knew just how angry she would be when she saw his house, his garden and his shabby suit.

" 'Oh, dear! Oh, dear! What shall I do?' wailed Mr. Rabbit, wringing his hands.

" 'Get busy and clean up,' advised Mr. Woodchuck, hurrying about his own work.

"Now Mr. Woodchuck was a worker and very, very neat. He meant to have his home looking just as fine as he could make it. He brought up some clean yellow sand from deep down in the ground and sprinkled it smoothly over his doorstep.

" 'I'll help you, if I get through my own work in time,' shouted Mr. Woodchuck over his shoulder.

"That gave Mr. Rabbit an idea. He would ask all his neighbors to help him, and perhaps then he could get his house and garden in order by the time Old Mother Nature arrived. So Mr. Rabbit called on Mr. Skunk and Mr. Coon and

Mr. Mink and Mr. Squirrel and Mr. Chipmunk, and all the rest of his neighbors, telling them of his trouble and asking them to help. Now, in spite of the trouble Mr. Rabbit was forever making for other people by his dreadful curiosity and meddling with other people's affairs, all his neighbors had a warm place in their hearts for Mr. Rabbit, and they all promised that they would help him as soon as they had their own work finished.

"Instead of hurrying home and getting to work himself, Mr. Rabbit stopped a while after each call and sat with his arms folded, watching the one he was calling on work. Mr. Rabbit was very fond of sitting with folded arms. It was very comfortable. But this was no time to be doing it, and Mr. Skunk told him so.

" 'If you want the rest of us to help

you, you'd better get things started your-self,' said old Mr. Skunk, carefully comb-ing out his big, plumy tail.

"'That's right, Mr. Skunk! That's right!' said Mr. Rabbit, starting along briskly, just as if he was going to hurry right home and begin work that very instant.

"But half an hour later, when Mr. Skunk happened to pass the home of Mr. Chipmunk, there sat Mr. Rabbit with his arms folded, watching Mr. Chipmunk hurrying about as only Mr. Chipmunk can.

"Finally Mr. Rabbit had made the round of all his friends and neighbors, and he once more reached his tumble-down house. 'Oh, dear,' sighed Mr. Rabbit, as he looked at the tangle of brambles which almost hid the little old house, 'I never, never can clear away all this! It will be a lot easier to work

when all my friends are here to help.'
So he sighed once more and folded his
arms, instead of beginning work as he
should have done. And then, because
the sun was bright and warm, and he
was very, very comfortable, old Mr.
Rabbit began to nod, and presently he
was fast asleep.

"Now Old Mother Nature likes to
take people by surprise, and it happened
that she chose this very day to make
her promised visit. She was greatly
pleased with all she saw as she went
along, until she came to the home of
Mr. Rabbit.

"'Mercy me!' exclaimed Old Mother
Nature, throwing up her hands as she
saw the tumble-down house almost hidden by the brambles and weeds. 'Can
it be possible that any one really lives
here?'

Then, peering through the tangle of

brambles, she spied old Mr. Rabbit sitting on his broken-down doorstep with his arms folded and fast asleep.

"At first she was very indignant, oh very indignant, indeed! She decided that Mr. Rabbit should be punished very severely. But as she watched him sitting there, dreaming in the warm sunshine, her anger began to melt away. The fact is, Old Mother Nature was like all the rest of Mr. Rabbit's neighbors — she just couldn't help loving happy-go-lucky Mr. Rabbit in spite of all his faults. With a long stick she reached in and tickled the end of his nose.

"Mr. Rabbit sneezed, and this made him wake up. He yawned and blinked, and then his eyes suddenly flew wide open with fright. He had discovered Old Mother Nature frowning at him. She pointed a long forefinger at him and said:

'In every single blessed day
There's time for work and time for play.
Who folds his arms with work undone
Doth cheat himself and spoil his fun.'

" 'Hereafter, Mr. Rabbit, you and your children and your children's children will never again be able to sit with folded arms until you or they have learned to work.'

"And that is why Peter Rabbit cannot fold his arms and still lives in a tumble-down house among the brambles," concluded Grandfather Frog.

III

WHY UNC' BILLY POSSUM PLAYS DEAD

III

WHY UNC' BILLY POSSUM PLAYS DEAD

ONE thing puzzled Peter Rabbit and Johnny Chuck and Striped Chipmunk a great deal after they had come to know Unc' Billy Possum and his funny ways. They had talked it over and wondered and wondered about it, and tried to understand it, and even had asked Unc' Billy about it. Unc' Billy had just grinned and said that they would have to ask his mammy. Of course they couldn't do that, and Unc' Billy knew they couldn't, for Unc' Billy's mammy had died long before he even thought of coming up from Ol' Virginny to the Green Forest and the

Green Meadows where they lived. He said it just to tease them, and when he said it, he chuckled until they chuckled too, just as if it really were the best kind of a joke.

Now you know it always is the thing that you try and try to find out and can't find out that you most want to find out. It was just so with Peter Rabbit and Johnny Chuck and Striped Chipmunk. The more they talked about it, the more they wanted to know. Why was it that Unc' Billy Possum played dead instead of trying to run away when he was surprised by his enemies? They always tried to run away. So did everybody else of their acquaintance excepting Unc' Billy Possum.

"There must be a reason," said Peter gravely, as he pulled thoughtfully at one of his long ears.

"Of course there is a reason," asserted

Johnny Chuck, chewing the end of a blade of grass.

"There's a reason for everything," added Striped Chipmunk, combing out the hair of his funny little tail.

"Then of course Grandfather Frog knows it," said Peter.

"Of course! Why didn't we think of him before?" exclaimed the others.

"I'll beat you to the Smiling Pool!" shouted Peter.

Of course he did, for his legs are long and made for running, but Striped Chipmunk was not far behind. Johnny Chuck took his time, for he knew that he could not keep up with the others. Besides he was so fat that to run made him puff and blow. Grandfather Frog sat just as usual on his big green lily-pad, and he grinned when he saw who his visitors were, for he guessed right away what they had come for.

"Chug-a-rum! What is it you want to know now?" he demanded, before Peter could fairly get his breath.

"If you please, Grandfather Frog, we want to know why it is that Unc' Billy Possum plays dead," replied Peter as politely as he knew how.

Grandfather Frog chuckled. "Just to fool people, stupid!" said he.

"Of course we know that," replied Striped Chipmunk, "but what we want to know is how he ever found out that he could fool people that way, and how he knows that he will fool them."

"I suspect that his mammy taught him," said Grandfather Frog, with another chuckle way down deep in his throat.

"But who taught his mammy?" persisted Striped Chipmunk.

Grandfather Frog snapped at a foolish green fly, and when it was safely tucked

away inside his white and yellow waistcoat, he turned once more to his three
little visitors, and there was a twinkle
in his big, goggly eyes.

"I see," said he, "that you *will* have
a story, and I suppose that the sooner
I tell it to you, the sooner you will
leave me in peace. Unc' Billy Possum's
grandfather a thousand times removed
was ———"

"Was this way back in the days when
the world was young?" interrupted Peter.

Grandfather Frog scowled at Peter.
"If I have any more interruptions, there
will be no story to-day," said he severely.

Peter looked ashamed and promised
that he would hold his tongue right
between his teeth until Grandfather Frog
was through. Grandfather Frog cleared
his throat and began again.

"Unc' Billy Possum's grandfather a
thousand times removed was very much

as Unc' Billy is now, only he was a little more spry and knew better than to stuff himself so full that he couldn't run. He was always very sly, and he played a great many tricks on his neighbors, and sometimes he got them into trouble. But when he did, he always managed to keep out of their way until they had forgotten all about their anger.

"One morning the very imp of mischief seemed to get into old Mr. Possum's head. Yes, Sir, it certainly did seem that way. And when you see Mischief trotting along the Lone Little Path, if you look sharp enough, you'll see Trouble following at his heels like a shadow. I never knew it to fail. It's just as sure as a stomach-ache is to follow over-eating."

Just here Grandfather Frog paused and looked very hard at Peter Rabbit. But Peter pretended not to notice, and after

slowly winking one of his big, goggly
eyes at Johnny Chuck, Grandfather Frog
continued:

"Anyway, as I said before, the imp of
mischief seemed to be in old Mr. Possum's
head that morning, for he began to play
tricks on his neighbors as soon as they
were out of bed. He hid Old King Bear's
breakfast, while the latter had his head
turned, and then pretended that he had
just come along. He was very polite
and offered to help Old King Bear hunt
for his lost breakfast. Then, whenever
Old King Bear came near the place where
it was hidden, old Mr. Possum would
hide it somewhere else. Old King Bear
was hungry, and he worked himself up
into a terrible rage, for he was in a hurry
for his breakfast. Old Mr. Possum was
very sympathetic and seemed to be doing his very best to find the lost meal.
At last Old King Bear turned his head

suddenly and caught sight of old Mr. Possum hiding that breakfast in a new place. My, my, but his temper did boil over! It certainly did. And if he could have laid hands on old Mr. Possum that minute, it surely would have been the end of him.

"But old Mr. Possum was mighty spry, and he went off through the Green Forest laughing fit to kill himself. Pretty soon he met Mr. Panther. He was very polite to Mr. Panther. He told him that he had just come from a call on Old King Bear, and hinted that Old King Bear was then enjoying a feast and that there might be enough for Mr. Panther, if he hurried up there at once.

"Now, Mr. Panther was hungry, for he had found nothing for his breakfast that morning. So he thanked old Mr. Possum and hurried away to find Old

King Bear and share in the good things old Mr. Possum had told about.

"Old Mr. Possum himself hurried on, chuckling as he thought of the way Mr. Panther was likely to be received, with Old King Bear in such a temper. Pretty soon along came Mr. Lynx. Old Mr. Possum told him the same story he had told Mr. Panther, and Mr. Lynx went bounding off in a terrible hurry, for fear that he would not be in time to share in that good breakfast. It was such a good joke that old Mr. Possum tried it on Mr. Wolf and Mr. Fisher and Mr. Fox. In fact, he hunted up every one he could think of and sent them to call on Old King Bear, and without really telling them so, he made each one think that he would get a share in that breakfast.

"Now, there wasn't any more breakfast than Old King Bear wanted himself.

and by the time Mr. Panther arrived, there wasn't so much as a crumb left. Then, one after another, the others came dropping in, each licking his chops, and all very polite to Old King Bear. At first he didn't know what to make of it, but pretty soon Mr. Fox delicately hinted that they had come in response to the invitation sent by Mr. Possum, and that as they were all very hungry, they would like to know when the feast would be ready. Right away Old King Bear knew that old Mr. Possum had been up to some of his tricks, and he told his visitors that they were the victims of a practical joke.

"My, my, my, how angry everybody grew! With Old King Bear at their head, they started out to hunt for old Mr. Possum. When he saw them coming, he realized that what he had thought was a joke had become no longer a laughing

matter for him. He was too frightened
to run, so he scrambled up a tree. He
quite forgot that Mr. Panther and Mr.
Lynx could climb just as fast as he. Up
the tree after him they scrambled, and
he crept as far out as he could get on
one of the branches. Mr. Panther didn't
dare go out there, so he just shook the
branch. He shook and shook and shook
and shook, and the first thing old Mr.
Possum knew, he was flying through the
air down to where the others were all ready
to pounce on him.

"Old Mr. Possum was frightened almost
to death. He shut his eyes, and then
he landed with a thump that knocked all
the wind from his body. When he got
his breath again, he still kept his eyes
closed, for he couldn't bear the thought
of looking at the cruel teeth and claws
of Old King Bear and the others. Presently, while he was wondering why they

didn't jump on him and tear him to pieces, Old King Bear spoke:

" 'I guess Mr. Possum won't play any more jokes, Mr. Panther,' said he. 'You just knocked the life out of him when you shook him off that branch.'

"Mr. Panther came over and sniffed at Mr. Possum and turned him over with one paw. All the time Mr. Possum lay just as if he were dead, because he was too frightened to move. 'I didn't mean to kill him,' said Mr. Panther. 'We certainly will miss him. What will we do with him?'

" 'Leave him here as a warning to others,' growled Old King Bear.

"Each in turn came up and sniffed of Mr. Possum, and then they all went about their business. He waited long enough to make sure that they were out of sight, and then took the shortest way home. When he got there and thought

It all over, he thought that the best joke of all was the way he had made everybody think that he was dead. And then a bright idea struck him: he would try the same trick whenever he was caught. So the next time he got in trouble, instead of running away, he tried playing dead. It was such a success that he taught his children how to do it, and they taught their children, and so on down to Unc' Billy, whom you know. Unc' Billy says it is a lot easier than running away, and safer, too. Besides, it is always such a joke. Now, don't bother me any more, for I want to take a nap," concluded Grandfather Frog.

"Thank you!" cried Peter Rabbit and Johnny Chuck and Striped Chipmunk, and started off to hunt up Unc' Billy Possum.

IV

WHY REDDY FOX WEARS RED

IV

WHY REDDY FOX WEARS RED

PETER RABBIT sat in the middle of the dear Old Briar-patch making faces and laughing at Reddy Fox. Of course that wasn't a nice thing to do, not a bit nice. But Peter had just had a narrow escape, a very narrow escape, for Reddy Fox had sprung out from behind a bush as Peter came down the Lone Little Path, and had so nearly caught Peter that he had actually pulled some fur out of Peter's coat. Now Peter was safe in the dear Old Briar-patch. He was a little out of breath, because he had had to use his long legs as fast as he knew how, but he was safe. You see, Reddy Fox wouldn't run the risk of tearing his handsome red coat on the brambles. Besides, they scratched terribly.

"Never mind, Peter Rabbit, I'll get you yet!" snarled Reddy, as he gave up and started back for the Green Forest.

"Reddy Fox is very sly!
Reddy Fox is very spry!
But sly and spry, 'tis vain to try
To be as sly and spry as I."

When Peter Rabbit shouted this, Reddy looked back and showed all his teeth, but Peter only laughed, and Reddy trotted on. Peter watched him out of sight.

"My! I wish I had such a handsome coat," he said, with a long sigh, for you know Peter's coat is very plain, very plain, indeed.

"You wouldn't, if you had to wear it for the same reason that Reddy Fox has to wear his. A good heart and honest

ways are better than fine clothes, Peter
Rabbit."

Peter looked up.   There was saucy,
pert, little Jenny Wren fussing around in
one of the old bramble bushes.

"Hello, Jenny!" said Peter.   "Why
does Reddy wear a red coat?"

"Do you mean to say that you don't
know?"   Jenny Wren looked very hard
at Peter with her sharp eyes.   "I thought
everybody knew that!   You certainly are
slow, Peter Rabbit.   I haven't time to
tell you about it now.   Go ask Grandfather Frog; he knows all about it."
Jenny Wren bustled off before Peter
could find his tongue.

Now, you all know how full of curiosity
Peter Rabbit is.   Jenny Wren's busy
tongue had set that curiosity fairly boil-
ing over.   He just couldn't sit still for
wondering and wondering why Reddy
Fox wears a red coat.   He had never

thought anything about it before, but now he couldn't get it out of his head. He just *had* to know. So, making sure that Reddy Fox had disappeared in the Green Forest, Peter started for the Smiling Pool, lipperty-lipperty-lip, as fast as he could go. There he found Grandfather Frog sitting on his big green lily-pad, just as usual.

"If you please, Grandfather Frog, why does Reddy Fox wear a red coat?" panted Peter, quite out of breath.

"Chug-a-rum!" grunted Grandfather Frog crossly. "Don't you know that it is very impolite to disturb people when they are having a nap?"

"I — I'm very sorry. Indeed I am, Grandfather Frog," said Peter very humbly. "Will you tell me if I come again some time when you are not so sleepy?"

Now, like everybody else, Grandfather

Frog is rather fond of Peter Rabbit, and now Peter looked so truly sorry, and at the same time there was such a look of disappointment in Peter's eyes, that Grandfather Frog forgot all about his crossness.

"Chug-a-rum!" said he. "You and your questions are a nuisance, Peter Rabbit, and I may as well get rid of you now as to have you keep coming down here and pestering me to death. Besides, any one who has to keep such a sharp watch for Reddy Fox as you do ought to know why he wears a red coat. If you'll promise to sit perfectly still and ask no foolish questions, I'll tell you the story."

Of course Peter promised, and settled himself comfortably to listen. And this is the story that Grandfather Frog told:

"A long time ago, when the world was young, old Mr. Fox, the grandfather a thousand times removed of Reddy Fox,

was one of the smartest of all the forest
and meadow people, just as Reddy is
now. He was so smart that he knew
enough not to appear smart, and the
fact is his neighbors thought him rather
dull. He wore just a common, every-
day suit of dull brown, like most of the
others, and there wasn't anything about
him to attract attention. He was always
very polite, very polite indeed, to every
one. Yes, Sir, Mr. Fox was very polite.
He always seemed to be minding his
own business, and he never went around
asking foolish questions or poking his
nose into other people's affairs."

Grandfather Frog stopped a minute
and looked very hard at Peter after he
said this, and Peter looked uncomfortable.

"Now, although Mr. Fox didn't appear to take any interest in other
people's affairs and never asked ques-

tions, he had two of the sharpest ears among all the little meadow and forest people, and while he was going about seeming to be just minding his own business, he was listening and listening to all that was said. Everything he heard he remembered, so that it wasn't long before he knew more about what was going on than all his neighbors together. But he kept his mouth tight closed, did Mr. Fox, and was very humble and polite to everybody. Every night he came home early and went to bed by sundown, and everybody said what good habits Mr. Fox had.

"But when everybody else was asleep, Mr. Fox used to steal out and be gone half the night. Yes, Sir, sometimes he'd be gone until almost morning. But he always took care to get home before any of his neighbors were awake, and then he'd wait until everybody was up before

he showed himself. When he came out
and started to hunt for his breakfast,
some one was sure to tell him of mischief done during the darkness of the
night. Sometimes it was a storehouse
broken into, and the best things taken.
Sometimes it was of terrible frights that
some of the littlest people had received
by being wakened in the night and
seeing a fierce face with long, sharp teeth
grinning at them. Sometimes it was of
worse things that were told in whispers.
Mr. Fox used to listen as if very much
shocked, and say that something ought
to be done about it, and wonder who it
could be who would do such dreadful
things.

"By and by things got so bad that
they reached the ears of Old Mother
Nature, and she came to find out what
it all meant. Now, the very night before
she arrived, Mrs. Quack, who lived on

the river bank, had a terrible fright.
Somebody sprang upon her as she was
sleeping, and in the struggle she lost all
her tail feathers. She hurried to tell Old
Mother Nature all about it, and big tears
rolled down her cheeks as she told how
she had lost all her beautiful tail feathers.
Mother Nature called all the people of the
forest and the meadows together. She
made them all pass before her, and she
looked sharply at each one as they went
by. Mr. Fox looked meeker than ever,
and he was very humble and polite.

"Now when Mr. Fox had paid his
respects and turned his back, Old Mother
Nature saw something red on the tail
of his coat. It was nothing but a little
smear of red clay, but that was enough
for Old Mother Nature. You see, she
knew that Mrs. Quack's home was right
at the foot of a red claybank. She didn't
say a word until everybody had paid

their respects and passed before her. Then she told them how grieved she was to hear of all the trouble there had been but that she couldn't watch over each one all the time; they must learn to watch out for themselves.

"And so that you may know who to watch out for, from now on never trust the one who wears a bright red coat," concluded Old Mother Nature.

"All of a sudden Mr. Fox became aware that everybody was looking at him, and in every face was hate. He glanced at his coat. It was bright red! Then Mr. Fox knew that he had been found out, and he sneaked away with his tail between his legs. The first chance he got, he went to Old Mother Nature and begged her to give him back his old coat. She promised that she would when his heart changed, and he changed his ways. But his heart never did change, and his children and his children's children were just like him. They have always been the smartest and the sliest and the most feared and disliked of all the little people on the meadows or in the forest. And now you know why Reddy Fox wears a red coat," concluded Grandfather Frog.

Peter Rabbit drew a long breath. "Thank you, thank you, Grandfather Frog!" said he. "I — I think hereafter I'll be quite content with my own suit, even if it isn't handsome. Jenny Wren was right. A good heart and honest ways are better than fine clothes."

V

WHY JIMMY SKUNK NEVER HURRIES

V

WHY JIMMY SKUNK NEVER HURRIES

THE Merry Little Breezes of Old Mother West Wind had just been released from the big bag in which she carries them every night to their home behind the Purple Hills and every morning brings them back to the Green Meadows to romp and play all day. They romped and raced and danced away, some one way, some another, to see whom they could find to play with. Presently some of them spied Jimmy Skunk slowly ambling down the Crooked Little Path, stopping every few steps to pull over a loose stone or stick. They knew what he was doing that for. They knew that he was looking for fat beetles for his breakfast. They danced over to him and formed a ring around him while they sang:

> "Who is it never, never hurries?
> Who is it never, never worries?
> Who is it does just what he pleases,
> Just like us Merry Little Breezes?
> Jimmy Skunk! Jimmy Skunk!"

Now not so far away but that he could hear them very plainly sat Peter Rabbit, just finishing his breakfast in a sweet-clover patch. He sat up very straight, so as to hear better. Of course some of the Merry Little Breezes saw him right away. They left Jimmy to come over and dance in a circle around Peter, for Peter is a great favorite with them. And as they danced they sang:

> "Who is it hops and skips and jumps?
> Who is it sometimes loudly thumps?
> Who is it dearly loves to play,
> But when there's danger runs away?
> Peter Rabbit! Peter Rabbit!"

Peter grinned good-naturedly. He is quite used to being laughed at for always running away, and he doesn't mind it in the least.

"When danger's near, who runs away will live to run another day," retorted Peter promptly. Then he began the maddest kind of a frolic with the Merry Little Breezes until they and he were quite tired out and ready for a good rest.

"I wish," said Peter, as he stretched himself out in the middle of the patch of sweet clover, "that you would tell me why it is that Jimmy Skunk never hurries."

"And we wish that you would tell us the same thing," cried one of the Merry Little Breezes.

"But I can't," protested Peter. "Everybody else seems to hurry, at times anyway, but Jimmy never does.

He says it is a waste of energy, whatever that means."

"I tell you what — let's go over to the Smiling Pool and ask Grandfather Frog about it now. He'll be sure to know," spoke up one of the Merry Little Breezes.

"All right," replied Peter, hopping to his feet. "But you'll have to ask him. I've asked him for so many stories that I don't dare ask for another right away, for fear that he will say that I am a nuisance."

So it was agreed that the Merry Little Breezes should ask Grandfather Frog why it is that Jimmy Skunk never hurries, and that Peter should keep out of sight until Grandfather Frog had begun the story, for they were sure that there would be a story. Away they all hurried to the Smiling Pool. The Merry Little Breezes raced so hard that they were quite out of breath when they burst through the bulrushes and surrounded Grandfather Frog, as he sat on his big green lily-pad.

"Oh, Grandfather Frog, why is it that Jimmy Skunk never hurries?" they panted.

"Chug-a-rum!" replied Grandfather Frog in his deepest, gruffest voice. "Chug-a-rum! Probably because he has learned better."

"Oh!" said one of the Merry Little Breezes, in a rather faint, disappointed sort of voice. Just then he spied a fat, foolish, green fly and blew it right over to Grandfather Frog, who snapped it up in a flash. Right away all the Merry Little Breezes began to hunt for foolish green flies and blow them over to Grandfather Frog, until he didn't have room for another one inside his white and yellow waistcoat. Indeed the legs of the last one he tried to swallow stuck out of one corner of his big mouth.

"Chug-a-rum!" said Grandfather Frog, trying very hard to get those legs out of sight. "Chug-a-rum! I always like to do something for those who do something for me, and I suppose now that I ought to tell you why it is that Jimmy Skunk never hurries. I would, if Peter Rabbit were here. If I tell you the story, Peter will be sure to hear of it, and then he will give me no peace until I tell it to him, and I don't like to tell stories twice."

"But he is here!" cried one of the Little Breezes. "He's right over behind that little clump of tall grass."

"Humph! I thought he wasn't very far away," grunted Grandfather Frog, with a twinkle in his great, goggly eyes.

Peter crept out of his hiding-place, looking rather shamefaced and very foolish. Then the Merry Little Breezes settled themselves on the lily-pads in a big circle around Grandfather Frog, and Peter sat down as close to the edge of the bank of the Smiling Pool as he dared to get. After what seemed to them a very long time, Grandfather Frog swallowed the legs of the last foolish green fly, opened his big mouth, and began:

"Of course you all know that long, long ago, when the world was young, things were very different from what they are now, very different indeed. The great-great-ever-so-great grandfather of Jimmy Skunk was slimmer and trimmer than Jimmy is. He was more like his cousins, Mr. Weasel and Mr. Mink. He was just as quick moving as they were. Yes, Sir, Mr. Skunk was very lively on his feet. He had to be to keep out of the way of his big neighbors, for in those days he didn't have

any means of protecting himself, as
Jimmy has now. He was dressed all in
black. You know it wasn't until Old
Mother Nature found out that he was
taking advantage of that black suit to
get into mischief on dark nights that she
gave him white stripes, so that the
darker the night, the harder it would be
for him to keep from being seen.

"Now Mr. Skunk was very smart and
shrewd, oh, very! When the hard times
came, which made so many changes in
the lives of the people who lived in the
Green Forest and on the Green Meadows,
Mr. Skunk was very quick to see that
unless he could think of some way to
protect himself, it was only a matter of
time when he would furnish a dinner
for one of his fierce big neighbors, and of
course Mr. Skunk had no desire to do
that. It was then that he asked Old
Mother Nature to give him a bag of

perfume so strong that it would make everybody ill but himself. Mother Nature thought it all over, and then she did, but she made him promise that he would never use it unless he was in great danger.

"Mr. Skunk had to try his new defence only once or twice before his enemies took the greatest care to let him alone. He found that he no longer had to run for a safe hiding-place when he met Mr. Wolf or Mr. Lynx or Mr. Panther. They just snarled at him and passed without offering to touch him. So Mr. Skunk grew very independent and went where he pleased when he pleased. And, because he no longer had to run from his enemies, he got out of the habit of running. Then he made a discovery. He watched those of his neighbors who were forever hurrying about looking for food, hurrying because all the time there was great fear upon them that an enemy might be near, hurrying because each was fearful that his neighbor would get more than he. It wasn't long before Mr. Skunk saw that in their hurry they overlooked a great deal. In fact, by just following after them slowly, he found all he wanted to eat.

"So Mr. Skunk began to grow fat. His neighbors, who were having hard work to make a living, grew envious, and said unkind things about him, and hinted that he must be stealing, or he never could have so much to eat. But Mr. Skunk didn't mind. He went right on about his business. He never worried, because, you know, he feared nobody. And he never hurried, because he found that it paid best to go slowly. In that way he never missed any of the good things that his hurrying, worrying neighbors did. So he grew fatter and fatter, while others grew thinner. After a while he almost forgot how to run. Being fat and never hurrying or worrying made him good-natured. He kept right on minding his own affairs and never meddling in the affairs of others, so that by and by his neighbors began to respect him.

"Of course he taught his children to do as he did, and they taught their children. And so, ever since that long-ago day, when the world was young, that little bag of perfume has been handed down in the Skunk family, and none of them has ever been afraid. Now you know why Jimmy Skunk, whom you all know, is so independent and never hurries."

"Thank you! Thank you, Grandfather Frog!" cried the Merry Little Breezes. "When you want some more foolish green flies, just let us know, and we'll get them for you."

"Chug-a-rum! What are you looking so wistful for, Peter Rabbit?" demanded Grandfather Frog.

"I — I was just wishing that I had a ——" began Peter. Then suddenly he made a face. "No, I don't either!" he declared. "I guess I'd better be getting home to the dear Old Briar-patch now. Mrs. Peter probably thinks something has happened to me." And away he went, lipperty-lipperty-lip.

VI

WHY SAMMY JAY HAS A FINE COAT

VI

SAMMY JAY has a very fine coat, a very beautiful coat. Everybody knows that. In fact, Sammy's coat has long been the envy of a great many of his neighbors in the Green Forest. Some of them, you know, have very modest coats. They are not beautiful at all. And yet the owners of some of these plain coats are among the most honest and hard-working of all the little people who live in the Green Forest. They find it hard, very hard indeed, to understand why such a scamp and mischiefmaker as Sammy Jay should be given such a wonderful blue coat with white trimmings.

Peter Rabbit often had thought about it. He has a number of feathered friends whom he likes ever so much better than he does Sammy Jay. In fact, he and Sammy are forever falling out, because Sammy delights to tease Peter. He sometimes makes up for it by warning Peter when Granny or Reddy Fox happens to be about, and Peter is honest enough to recognize this and put it to Sammy's credit. But in spite of this, it never seemed to him quite right that Sammy Jay should be so handsomely dressed.

"Of course," said Peter to Grandfather Frog, "Old Mother Nature knows a great deal more than I do ——"

"Really! You don't mean to say so! Chug-a-rum! You don't mean to say so, Peter!" interrupted Grandfather Frog, pretending to be very much surprised at what Peter said.

"You don't mean to say so, Peter," interrupted
Grandfather Frog.

Peter grinned and wrinkled his nose at Grandfather Frog.

"Yes," said he, "Old Mother Nature knows a great deal more than I do, but it seems to me as if she had made a mistake in giving Sammy Jay such a handsome coat. There must be a reason, I suppose, but for the life of me I cannot understand it. I should think that she would give such a thief as Sammy Jay the very homeliest suit she could find. You may depend I would, if I were in her place."

Grandfather Frog chuckled until he shook all over.

"It's lucky for some of us that you are not in her place!" said he. "Chug-a-rum! It certainly is lucky!"

"If I were, I would give you a handsome coat, too, Grandfather Frog," replied Peter.

Grandfather Frog suddenly swelled out

with indignation. "Chug-a-rum! Chug-a-rum! What's the matter with the coat I have got, Peter Rabbit? Tell me that! Who's got a handsomer one?" Grandfather Frog glared with his great, goggly eyes at Peter.

"I didn't mean to say that you haven't got a handsome coat. Your coat *is* handsome, very handsome indeed, Grandfather Frog," Peter hastened to say. "I always did like green. I just love it! And I should think you would be ever so proud of your white and yellow waistcoat. I would if it were mine. What I meant to say is, that if I were in Old Mother Nature's place, I would give some plain folks handsome suits. Certainly, I wouldn't give such a rascal as Sammy Jay one of the handsomest coats in all the Green Forest. Knowing Sammy as well as I do, it is hard work to believe that he came by it honestly."

Grandfather Frog chuckled way down deep in his throat.

"Sammy came by it honestly enough, Peter. Yes, Sir, he came by it honestly enough, because it was handed down to him by his father, who got it from his father, who got it from his father, and so on, way back to the days when the world was young, but —— " Grandfather Frog paused, and that dreamy, far-away look which Peter had seen so often came into his great, goggly eyes.

"But what, Grandfather Frog?" asked Peter eagerly, when he could keep still no longer.

Grandfather Frog settled himself comfortably on his big green lily-pad and looked very hard at Peter.

"I'm going to tell you a story, Peter Rabbit," said he, "so that never again will you be led to doubt that Old Mother Nature knows exactly what she is about.

In the first place, Sammy Jay is not wholly to blame for all his bad habits. Some of them were handed down to him with his fine coat, just the same as your troublesome curiosity was handed down to you with the white patch on the seat of your trousers."

Peter nodded. He had felt a great many times that he just couldn't help this habit of poking that wobbly little nose of his in where it had no business to be, any more than he could change that funny little bunch of white cotton, which he called a tail, for a really, truly tail.

"Of course, you have heard all about what a very fine gentleman Sammy Jay's great-great-ever-so-great grandfather was thought to be until it was discovered that he was all the time stealing from his neighbors and putting the blame on others, and how Old Mother Nature pun-

ished him by taking away the beautiful
voice of which he was so proud, and
giving him instead the harsh voice which
Sammy has now, and making him tell
just what he is by screaming 'thief, thief,
thief!' every time he opens his mouth
to speak.

"At first Old Mother Nature had intended to take away the fine coat of
which Mr. Jay was so proud, but when
he discovered that he had lost his fine
voice, he was so ashamed that he hurried
away to hide himself from the eyes of
his neighbors, so that Old Mother Nature
didn't have time to change his coat just
then.

"'I'll wait a bit,' said she to herself,
'and see how he behaves. Perhaps he is
truly sorry for what he has done, and
I will not have to punish him more.'

"But if Mr. Jay was truly sorry, he
gave no signs of it. You see, he had

cheated his neighbors, and had stolen from them for so long, that he found this the easiest way to get a living. His bad habits had become fixed, as bad habits have a way of doing. Besides, right down in his heart, he wasn't sorry for what he had done, only angry at having been found out. Now that he had been found out, of course every one was on the watch for him, and it wasn't so easy to steal as it had been before. So now, instead of going about openly, with his head held high, he grew very crafty, and sneaked quietly about through the Green Forest, trying to keep out of sight, that he might the easier steal from his neighbors and make trouble for them.

"When Old Mother Nature saw this, she changed her mind about taking away his handsome suit. 'If I do that,' thought she, 'it will make it all the easier for him to keep out of sight, and all the harder for his neighbors to know when he is about.'

"So instead of giving him the plain, homely suit that she had thought of giving him, she made his coat of blue brighter than before and trimmed it with the whitest of white trimmings, so that Mr. Jay had one of the very handsomest coats in all the Green Forest. At first he was very proud of it, but it wasn't long before he found that it was very hard work to keep out of sight when he wanted to. That bright blue coat was forever giving him away when he was out on mischief. Everybody was all the time on the watch for it, and so where in the past Mr. Jay had been able, without any trouble, to steal all he wanted to eat, now he sometimes actually had to work for his food, and get it honestly or else go hungry.

"You would suppose that he would

have mended his ways, wouldn't you?"

Peter nodded.

"But he didn't. He grew more sly and crafty than ever. But in spite of this, he didn't begin to make as much trouble as before. He couldn't, you know, because of his bright coat. When Old Mother Nature found that Mr. Jay had passed along his bad habits to his children, she passed along his handsome blue coat, too, and so it has been from that long-ago day right down to this. Sammy Jay's fine coat isn't a reward for goodness, as is Winsome Bluebird's, but is to help the other little people of the Green Forest and the Green Meadows to protect themselves, and keep track of Sammy when he is sneaking and snooping around looking for mischief. Now what do you think, Peter Rabbit?"

Peter scratched one long ear and then the other long ear thoughtfully, and he looked a wee bit ashamed as he replied: "I guess Old Mother Nature makes no mistakes and always knows just what she is doing."

"Chug-a-rum!" said Grandfather Frog in his deepest voice. "You may be sure she does. And another thing, Peter Rabbit: Never judge any one by his clothes. It is a great mistake, a very great mistake. Plain clothes sometimes cover the kindest hearts, and fine clothes often are a warning to beware of mischief."

"I — I don't know but you are right," admitted Peter.

"I know I am," said Grandfather Frog.

VII

WHY JERRY MUSKRAT BUILDS HIS HOUSE IN THE WATER

VII

WHY JERRY MUSKRAT BUILDS HIS HOUSE
IN THE WATER

PETER RABBIT and Johnny Chuck
had gone down to the Smiling Pool
for a call on their old friend, Jerry
Muskrat. But Jerry was nowhere to be
seen. They waited and waited, but no
Jerry Muskrat.

"Probably he is taking a nap in that
big house of his," said Johnny Chuck,
"and if he is we'll have to sit here until
he wakes up, or else go back home and
visit him some other time."

"That's so," replied Peter. "I don't
see what he has his house in the water
for, anyway. If he had built it on land,
like sensible people, we might be able to

waken him. Funny place to build a house, isn't it?"

Johnny Chuck scratched his head thoughtfully. "It does seem a funny place," he admitted. "It certainly does seem a funny place. But then, Jerry Muskrat is a funny fellow. You know how much of the time he stays in the water. That seems funny to me. I suppose there is a reason for it, and probably there is a reason for building his house where it is. I've found that there is a reason for most things. Probably Jerry's great-great-grandfather built his house that way, and so Jerry does the same thing."

Peter Rabbit suddenly brightened up. "I do believe you are right, Johnny Chuck, and if you are, there must be a story about it, and if there is a story, Grandfather Frog will be sure to know it. There he is, over on his big green lily-pad, and he looks as if he might be feeling very good-natured this morning. Let's go ask him why Jerry Muskrat builds his house in the water."

Grandfather Frog saw them coming, and he guessed right away that they were coming for a story. He grinned to himself and pretended to go to sleep.

"Good morning, Grandfather Frog," said Johnny Chuck. Grandfather Frog didn't answer. Johnny tried again, and still no reply.

"He's asleep," said Johnny, looking dreadfully disappointed, "and I guess we'd better not disturb him, for he might wake up cross, and of course we wouldn't get a story if he did."

Peter looked at Grandfather Frog sharply. He wasn't so sure that that was a real nap. It seemed to him that there was just the least little hint of a smile in the corners of Grandfather

Frog's big mouth. "You sit here a minute," he whispered in Johnny Chuck's ear.

So Johnny Chuck sat down where he was, which was right where Grandfather Frog could see him by lifting one eyelid just the teeniest bit, and Peter hopped along the bank until he was right behind Grandfather Frog. Now just at that place on the bank was growing a toad-stool. Peter looked over at Johnny Chuck and winked. Then he turned around, and with one of his long hind-feet, he kicked the toadstool with all his might. Now toadstools, as you all know, are not very well fastened at the roots, and this one was no different from the rest. When Peter kicked it it flew out into the air and landed with a great splash in the Smiling Pool, close beside the big green lily-pad on which Grandfather Frog was sitting. Of course he didn't see it coming, and of course it gave him a great start.

"Chug-a-rum!" exclaimed Grandfather Frog and dived head first into the water. A minute later Peter's sharp eyes saw him peeping out from under a lily-pad to see what had frightened him so.

"Ha, ha, ha!" shouted Peter, dancing about on the bank. "Ha, ha, ha! Grandfather Frog, afraid of a toadstool! Ha, ha, ha!"

At first Grandfather Frog was angry, very angry indeed. But he is too old and too wise to lose his temper for long over a joke, especially when he has been fairly caught trying to play a joke himself. So presently he climbed back on to his big green lily-pad, blinking his great, goggly eyes and looking just a wee bit foolish.

"Chug-a-rum! I might have known that that was some of your work, Peter

Rabbit," said he, "but I thought it surely was a stone thrown by Farmer Brown's boy. What do you mean by frightening an old fellow like me this way?"

"Just trying to get even with you for trying to fool us into thinking that you were asleep when you were wide awake," replied Peter. "Oh, Grandfather Frog, do tell us why it is that Jerry Muskrat builds his house in the water. Please do!"

"I have a mind not to, just to get even with you," said Grandfather Frog, settling himself comfortably, "but I believe I will, to show you that there are some folks who can take a joke without losing their temper."

"Goody!" cried Peter and Johnny Chuck together, sitting down side by side on the very edge of the bank.

Grandfather Frog folded his hands

across his white and yellow waistcoat and half closed his eyes, as if looking way, way back into the past.

"Chug-a-rum!" he began. "A long, long time ago, when the world was young, there was very little dry land, and most of the animals lived in the water. Yes, Sir, most of the animals lived in the water, as sensible animals do to-day."

Peter nudged Johnny Chuck. "He means himself and his family," he whispered with a chuckle.

"After a time," continued Grandfather Frog, "there began to be more land and still more. Then some of the animals began to spend most of their time on the land. As there got to be more and more land, more and more of the animals left the water, until finally most of them were spending nearly all of the time on land. Now Old Mother

Nature had been keeping a sharp watch, as she always does, and when she found that they were foolish enough to like the land best, she did all that she could to make things comfortable for them. She taught them how to run and jump and climb and dig, according to which things they liked best to do, so that it wasn't very long before a lot of them forgot that they ever had lived in the water, and they began to look down on those who still lived in the water, and to put on airs and hold their heads very high.

"Now, of course, Old Mother Nature didn't like this, and to punish them she said that they should no longer be able to live in the water, even if they wanted to. At first they only laughed, but after a while they found that quite often there were times when it would be very nice to be at home in the water as they once had been. But it was of no use. Some could swim as long as they could keep their heads above water, but as soon as they put their heads under water they were likely to drown. You know that is the way with you to-day, Peter Rabbit."

Peter nodded. He knew that he could swim if he had to, but only for a very little way, and he hated the thought of it.

"Now there were a few animals, of whom old Mr. Muskrat, the grandfather a thousand times removed of Jerry Muskrat, was one, who learned to walk and run on dry land, but who still loved the water," continued Grandfather Frog. "One day Old Mother Nature found Mr. Muskrat sitting on a rock, looking very mournful.

" 'What's the matter, Mr. Muskrat?' she asked.

"Mr. Muskrat looked very much

ashamed as he finally owned up that he
was envious of his cousins and some of
the other animals, because they had
such fine houses on the land.

"'Then why don't you build you a
fine house on the land?' asked Old
Mother Nature.

"Mr. Muskrat hesitated. 'I — I —
love the water too well to want to stay
on land all the time,' said he, 'and —
and — well, I was put in the water in
the first place, and I ought to be contented with what I have got and make
the best of it.'

"Old Mother Nature was so pleased
with Mr. Muskrat's reply that right
away she made up her mind that he
should have a finer house than any of
the others, so she took him over to a
quiet little pool, where the water was
not too deep and she showed him how
to build a wonderful house of mud and

rushes and twigs, with a nice warm bedroom lined with grass above the water, and an entrance down under the water, so that no one except those who still lived most of the time in the water could possibly get into it. None of his friends on land had such a big, fine house, and Mr. Muskrat was very proud of it. But with all his pride he never forgot that it was a reward for trying to be content with his surroundings and making the best of them.

"So from that day to this, the Muskrats have built their houses in the water, and have been among the most industrious, contented, and happy of all the animals. And that is why Jerry Muskrat has built that fine house in the Smiling Pool and has so few enemies," concluded Grandfather Frog.

Peter Rabbit drew a long breath, which was almost a sigh. "I almost wish my grandfather a thousand times removed had been content to stay in the water, too," he said.

"Chug-a-rum!" retorted Grandfather Frog. "If he had, you wouldn't have the dear Old Briar-patch. Be content with what you've got."

"I think I will," said Peter.

VIII

WHY OLD MAN COYOTE HAS MANY VOICES

VIII

OF course Old Man Coyote has only one voice, but that one is such a wonderful voice that he can make it sound like a great many voices, all yelping and howling and shouting and laughing at the same time. So those who hear him always say that he has many voices, and that certainly is the way it seems. The first time Peter Rabbit heard Old Man Coyote, he was sure, absolutely sure, that there was a whole crowd of strangers on the Green Meadows, and you may be sure that he kept very close to his dear Old Briar-patch. If you had been there and tried to tell Peter that all that noise was made by just one voice, he wouldn't have believed you. No, Sir, he wouldn't have believed you. And you couldn't have blamed him.

It was the Merry Little Breezes of Old Mother West Wind who first told Peter who the stranger was and warned him to watch out, because Old Man Coyote is just as fond of Rabbit as Granny or Reddy Fox, and is even more crafty and sly than they. Peter thanked the Merry Little Breezes for the warning, and then he asked them how many of his family Old Man Coyote had brought with him. Of course the Merry Little Breezes told Peter that Old Man Coyote was all alone, and they became very indignant when Peter laughed at them. He just couldn't help it.

"Why," said he, "every night I hear a whole crowd yelping and howling together."

"But you don't!" insisted the Merry Little Breezes. "It is Old Man Coyote alone who makes all that noise."

"Don't you suppose I know what I hear?" demanded Peter.

"No!" retorted the Merry Little Breezes. "You may have big ears and be able to hear a great deal, sometimes a great deal more than you have any business to hear, but you are old enough by this time to have learned that you cannot believe all you hear." And with that the Merry Little Breezes indignantly raced away to spread the news all over the Green Meadows.

Now Peter was quite as indignant because they thought he couldn't or shouldn't believe his own ears, as they were because he wouldn't believe what they told him, and all the rest of that day he couldn't put the matter out of his mind. He was still thinking of it

as the Black Shadows came creeping
down from the Purple Hills across the
Green Meadows. Suddenly Peter saw a
dark form skulking among the Black
Shadows. At first he thought it was
Reddy Fox, only somehow it looked
bigger. Peter, safe in the dear Old
Briar-patch, watched. Presently the
dark form came out from among the
Black Shadows where Peter could see
it clearly, sat down, pointed a sharp
nose up at the first twinkling little stars,
opened a big mouth, and out of it poured
such a yelping and howling as made
Peter shiver with fright. And now Peter
had to believe his eyes rather than his
ears. His ears told him that there were
many voices, but his eyes told him that
all that dreadful sound was coming out
of one mouth. It was hard, very hard,
to believe, but it was so.

"The Merry Little Breezes were

right," muttered Peter to himself, as Old Man Coyote trotted away in the direction of the Green Forest, and he felt a wee bit ashamed to think that he had refused to believe them.

After that, Peter could think of nothing but Old Man Coyote's wonderful voice that sounded like many voices, and at the very first opportunity he hurried over to the Smiling Pool to ask Grandfather Frog what it meant.

"Chug-a-rum!" said Grandfather Frog. "It means simply that Old Man Coyote comes of a very smart family, and that he knows how to make the most of the gift of Old Mother Nature to his grandfather a thousand times removed."

This sounded so much like a story that Peter straightway teased Grandfather Frog to tell him all about it. At last, to get rid of him and enjoy a little quiet and peace, Grandfather Frog did so.

"Chug-a-rum!" he began, as he always does. "The great-great-ever-so-great grandfather of Old Man Coyote, who lived long, long ago when the world was young, was very much as Old Man Coyote is to-day. He was just as smart and just as clever. Indeed, he was smart enough and clever enough not to let his neighbors know that he was smart and clever at all. Those were very peaceful times at first, and everybody was on the best of terms with everybody else, as you know. There was plenty to eat without the trouble to steal, and everybody was honest simply because it was easier to be honest than it was to be dishonest. So Old King Bear ruled in the Green Forest, and everybody was happy and contented.

"But there came a time when food

was scarce, and it was no longer easy
to get plenty to eat. It was then that
the stronger began to steal from the
weaker, and by and by even to prey
upon those smaller than themselves.
The times grew harder and harder, and
because hunger is a hard and cruel
master, it made the larger and stronger
people hard and cruel, too. Some of
them it made very sly and cunning, like
old Mr. Fox. Mr. Coyote was another
whom it made sly and cunning. He was
smart in the first place, even smarter
than Mr. Fox, and he very early made
up his mind that if he would live, it
must be by his wits, for he wasn't big
enough or strong enough to fight with
his neighbors such as his big cousin,
Mr. Timber Wolf, or Mr. Lynx, or Mr.
Panther or Old King Bear, who was
king no longer. And yet he liked the
same things to eat.

"So he used to study and plan how he could outwit them without danger to himself. 'A whole skin is better than a full stomach, but both a whole skin and a full stomach are better still,' said he to himself, as he thought and schemed. For a while he was content to catch what he could without danger to himself, and to eat what his bigger and stronger neighbors left when they happened to get more than they wanted for themselves. Little by little he got the habit of slyly following them when they were hunting, always keeping out of sight. In this way, he managed to get many meals of scraps. But these scraps never wholly satisfied him, and his mouth used to water as he watched the others feast on the very best when they had had a successful hunt. He knew it wouldn't be of the least use to go out and boldly ask for some, for in those hard times everybody was very, very selfish.

"The times grew harder and harder, until it seemed as if Old Mother Nature had wholly forgotten her little people of the Green Meadows and the Green Forest. Mr. Coyote still managed to pick up a living, but he was hungry most of the time, and the less he had to put in his stomach, the sharper his wits grew. At last one day, as he stole soft-footed through the Green Forest, he discovered Mr. Lynx having a great feast. To keep still and watch him was almost more than Mr. Coyote could stand, for he was so hungry that it seemed as if the sides of his stomach almost met, it was so empty.

"'If I could make myself into three, we could take that dinner away from Mr. Lynx!' thought he, and right on top of that thought came a great idea.

Why not make Mr. Lynx think he had a lot of friends with him? It would do no harm to try. So Mr. Coyote put his nose up in the air and howled. Mr. Lynx looked up and grinned. He had no fear of Mr. Coyote. Then Mr. Coyote hurried around to the other side of Mr. Lynx, all the time keeping out of sight, and howled again, and this time he tried to make his voice sound different. Mr. Lynx stopped eating and looked up a little surprised. 'I wonder if Mr. Coyote has got a brother with him,' thought he. A minute later Mr. Coyote howled again from the place where he had howled in the first place. 'He certainly has,' thought Mr. Lynx, 'but I'm a match for two of them,' and once more he went on eating.

"Then Mr. Coyote began to run in a circle around Mr. Lynx, always keeping out of sight in the thick brush, and every few steps he yelped or howled, and each yelp or howl he tried to make sound different. Now Mr. Coyote could run very fast, and he ran now as hard as ever he could in a big circle, yelping and howling and making his voice sound as different as possible each time. Mr. Lynx grew anxious and lost his appetite. 'Mr. Coyote must have a whole crowd of brothers,' thought he. 'I guess this is no place for me!' With that he started to sneak away.

"Mr. Coyote followed him, still trying to make his voice sound like the voices of many. Mr. Lynx gave a hurried look over his shoulder and began to run. Mr. Coyote kept after him, yelping and howling, until he was sure that Mr. Lynx was so frightened that he wouldn't dare come back. Then Mr. Coyote returned to the dinner Mr. Lynx had left, and ate and ate until he couldn't hold another mouthful. His throat was very raw and sore because he had strained it trying to make his voice change so often, but he didn't mind this, because, you know, it felt so good to have all he could eat at one time once more.

"Now it just happened that Old Mother Nature had come along just in time to see and hear Mr. Coyote, and it tickled her so to think that Mr. Coyote had been so smart that what do you think she did? Why, while he slept that night, she healed his sore throat, and she gave him a new voice; and this voice was very wonderful, for it sounded for all the world like many voices, all yelping and howling at the same time. After that, all Mr. Coyote had to do when he wanted to frighten some one bigger and stronger than himself was to open his mouth and send forth his new voice, which sounded like many voices.

"So he had plenty to eat from that time on. And all his children and his children's children had that same wonderful voice, just as Old Man Coyote has now. Chug-a-rum! Now scamper home, Peter Rabbit, and see that you don't let Old Man Coyote's sharp wits get you into trouble."

"Thank you, Grandfather Frog!" cried Peter and scampered as fast as he could go for the dear, safe Old Briar-patch.

IX

WHY MINER, THE MOLE LIVES UNDER GROUND

IX

STRIPED CHIPMUNK sat staring at a little ridge where the grass was raised up   He had often seen little ridges like that without thinking much about them.   He knew that they were made by Miner the Mole.   He had known that ever since he was big enough to begin to ask questions.   But now as he looked at this one, it suddenly struck him that he had not seen Miner the Mole more than once or twice in all his life.

"What a queer way of living!" thought Striped Chipmunk.   "It's all very well to have a snug house under the ground.

where one can sleep the long cold winter away and be perfectly safe, but what any one wants to live under the ground all the time for, in the beautiful spring-time and summertime and autumntime, I can't understand. Just think of all that Miner misses — the sunshine, the flowers, the songs of the birds, and the Merry Little Breezes to play with! I wonder ——"

"What do you wonder?" The voice was so close to Striped Chipmunk that it made him jump. He whirled about. There was Johnny Chuck, who had tip-toed up as softly as he knew how, to give Striped Chipmunk a scare. Johnny grinned. "What do you wonder?" he repeated.

Striped Chipmunk made a face at Johnny. "I wonder something that I bet you don't know," he replied.

"That's easy," replied Johnny.

"There are more things I don't know than I do know, but I'm always ready to learn. What is it this time?"

"Why does Miner the Mole live under ground all the time?" Striped Chipmunk pointed to the ridge made by Miner.

Johnny Chuck scratched his head thoughtfully.

"I don't know," he confessed finally. "I never thought of it before. Of course there must be a reason. He never comes out to play with the rest of us — just spends all his time by himself down in the dark, digging and digging. I wonder ——"

"Well, what do *you* wonder?"

"The same thing you wonder," laughed Johnny Chuck. "If you haven't got anything else to do, let's go down to the Smiling Pool and ask Grandfather Frog; he'll be sure to know."

Striped Chipmunk hadn't anything else to do, so off they started. On the way they met Jimmy Skunk and Danny Meadow Mouse. Neither of them knew why Miner the Mole lives under ground, and because they hadn't anything better to do, they also started for the Smiling Pool.

Grandfather Frog was sitting on his big green lily-pad in the warm sunshine, and for once he didn't have to be teased for a story.

"Chug-a-rum!" said he in his deep voice. "It's very strange to me how little some folks know about their nearest neighbors." He looked up and winked at jolly, round, bright Mr. Sun.

Striped Chipmunk, Johnny Chuck, Jimmy Skunk, and Danny Meadow Mouse looked as though they felt very foolish, as indeed they did. You see, all their lives Miner the Mole had been one of their nearest neighbors, and yet they didn't know the first thing about him.

"It happened a long time ago," continued Grandfather Frog.

"When the world was young?" interrupted Danny Meadow Mouse.

"Of course," replied Grandfather Frog, pretending to be very much put out at such a foolish question. Danny hung his head and resolved that he would bite his tongue before he asked another question.

"In those days Miner's great-great-grandfather a thousand times removed didn't live under ground," continued Grandfather Frog. "Nobody did. He wasn't so very different from a lot of other animals. Food was plenty, and everybody was on the best of terms with everybody else. Mr. Mole lived just as the rest did. He went and came as he pleased, and enjoyed the sunshine and took part in all the good times of his neighbors. Everybody liked him, and whenever he made a call, he was sure of a welcome. But one thing Mr. Mole never did; he never meddled in other people's affairs. No, Sir, Mr. Mole never poked his nose in where he had no business.

"For a long time everything went smoothly with all the people of the Green Forest and the Green Meadows. Then came hard times. They grew harder and harder. Food was scarce and kept growing more scarce. Everybody was hungry, and you know how it is with hungry people — they grow ugly and quarrelsome. Matters grew worse and worse, and then it was that fear was born. The big people, like Old King Bear and Mr. Wolf and Mr. Panther and Mr. Lynx, began to look with hungry eyes on the little people, and the little people began to grow afraid and hide from the big people, and all the time they were continually quarreling among themselves and stealing from each other to get enough to eat.

"Now, as I said before, Mr. Mole never had meddled with other people's business, and he didn't now. He went off by himself to think things over. 'It isn't safe to run around any more,' said he. 'I met Mr. Wolf this morning, and he looked at me with such a hungry look in his eyes that it gave me the cold shivers. I believe he would have eaten me, if I hadn't crawled into an old hollow stump. Now I can't run fast, because my legs are too short. I can't climb trees like Mr. Squirrel, and I can't swim like Mr. Muskrat. The only thing I can do is to dig.'

"You see, Mr. Mole always had been

very fond of digging, and he had done so much of it that his front legs and claws had grown very stout.

" 'Now if I dig a hole and keep out of sight, I won't have to worry about Mr. Wolf or anybody else,' continued Mr. Mole to himself. So he went to work at once and dug a hole on the Green Meadows, and, because he wanted to be comfortable, he made a big hole. When it was finished, he was tired, so he curled up at the bottom for a nap. He was awakened by hearing voices outside. He knew those voices right away. They were the voices of Mr. Fox and Mr. Badger.

" 'These are terrible times,' said Mr. Fox. 'I'm so hungry that I'm wasting away to a shadow. I wonder who has dug this hole.'

" 'Mr. Mole,' replied Mr. Badger. 'I saw him at work here this morning.

Have you noticed how very plump he looks?'

" 'Yes,' replied Mr. Fox. 'He made my mouth water the very last time I saw him. Seems to me I can smell him now. If he had made this hole just a little bit bigger I would go down and pull him out, but I am too tired to do any digging now.'

" 'I tell you what,' replied Mr. Badger. 'We'll hunt together a little longer, and then if we can't find anything to eat, we'll come back, and I'll help you dig. I hate to hurt Mr. Mole, because he always minds his own business, but these are hard times, and each one must look out for himself.'

"With that they went away, leaving Mr. Mole shaking with fright at the bottom of his hole. 'It's of no use,' thought Mr. Mole. 'If I go outside, they will soon find me, and if I stay here, they will dig me out. Oh, dear, oh, dear! What ever can I do?'

"He lay there feeling very helpless and miserable, when all of a sudden a thought came to him. If he had made his hole small, just big enough for him to crawl into, Mr. Badger and Mr. Fox would have had to do a great deal of digging to make it big enough for either of them to get in! He would make a little tunnel off one side and hide in that. So he went to work and made a little tunnel off one side just big enough for him to squeeze into. He worked very hard and very fast, and by the time Mr. Badger and Mr. Fox returned, Mr. Mole was at the end of a long tunnel, so far from the hole he had first dug that he knew it would take them a long time to dig him out, even if they noticed his tunnel.

"But they didn't. They dug down to the bottom of his hole and then, because

they didn't find him there, they straightway fell to quarreling, each blaming the
other for suggesting such a lot of hard
work for nothing. Finally they went
away, still calling each other names, and
from that day to this, Foxes and Badgers
have never been friends.

"Mr. Mole was very thankful for his
narrow escape, and it set him to thinking.
If he had a lot of these underground
tunnels, no one would be able to catch
him. It was a splendid idea! He went
to work on it at once. And then he
made a discovery — such a splendid discovery! There was plenty of food to
eat right down under ground — worms
and grubs — all he needed. After that,
Mr. Mole spent all his time in his tunnels and seldom put his nose outside.
He was safe, and he was comfortable,
and he could always find something to
eat by digging for it.

"Little by little his old neighbors forgot all about him. Because he had little use for them, his eyes grew smaller and smaller, and when he did come up into the light, they hurt him so that he was glad to go back into the dark again. He was perfectly happy and satisfied there, and what is there in life better than to be happy and satisfied?"

"Nothing," replied Striped Chipmunk, at whom Grandfather Frog happened to be looking when he asked the question.

"Right!" replied Grandfather Frog. "And now you know why Miner the Mole lives under ground — because he is perfectly happy and satisfied there."

Just then up came Peter Rabbit, all out of breath.

"Has Grandfather Frog been telling a story?" he panted.

"Yes," replied Striped Chipmunk, winking at Grandfather Frog, "and now we are going back home perfectly happy and satisfied."

And to this day Peter Rabbit wonders what the story was that he missed.

X

WHY MR. SNAKE CANNOT WINK

X

PETER RABBIT and Johnny Chuck were playing tag on the Green Meadows. Of course Peter can run so much faster than Johnny Chuck that he would never have been "it" if he had tried his best to keep out of the way. But he didn't. No, Sir, Peter Rabbit didn't do anything of the kind. He pretended that one of his long hind-legs was lame so that he had to run on three legs, while Johnny Chuck could use all four. It was great fun. They raced and dodged and twisted and turned. Sometimes Peter was so excited that he would forget and use all four legs. Then Johnny Chuck would shout "No fair!"

Peter would say that he didn't mean
to, and to make up for it would be "it"
and try to catch Johnny.

Now it happened that curled up on a
little grassy tussock, taking an early
morning sun-bath, lay little Mr. Greensnake.   Of course Peter Rabbit and
Johnny Chuck were not afraid of him.
If it had been Mr. Rattlesnake or Mr.
Gophersnake, it would have been different.   But from little Mr. Greensnake
there was nothing to fear, and sometimes,
just for fun, Peter would jump right over
him.   When he did that, Peter always
winked good-naturedly.   But Mr. Greensnake never winked back.   Instead he
would raise his head, run his tongue
out at Peter, and hiss in what he tried
to make a very fierce and angry manner.
Then Peter would laugh and wink at
him again.   But never once did Mr.
Greensnake wink back.

Peter was thinking of this as he and Johnny Chuck stretched out in a sunny spot to get their breath and rest. He had never thought of it before, but now that he had noticed it, he couldn't remember that he ever had seen little Mr. Greensnake wink, nor any of Mr. Greensnake's relatives. He mentioned the matter to Johnny Chuck.

"That's so," replied Johnny thought fully. "I never have seen any of them wink, either. Do you suppose they can wink?"

"Let's go ask Mr. Greensnake," said Peter.

Up they hopped and raced over to the grassy tussock where Mr. Greensnake lay, but to all their questions he would make no reply save to run out his tongue at them. Finally they gave up asking him.

"I tell you what, let's go over to the

Smiling Pool and ask Grandfather Frog.
He'll be sure to know, and perhaps, if
he is feeling good, he'll tell us a story,"
said Peter.

So off they scampered to the Smiling
Pool. There they found Grandfather
Frog sitting on his big green lily-pad
just as usual, and Peter knew by the look
in his great, goggly eyes that Grandfather
Frog had a good breakfast of foolish
green flies tucked away inside his white
and yellow waistcoat. His eyes twinkled
as Peter and Johnny very politely wished
him good morning.

"Good morning," said he gruffly.

But Peter had seen that twinkle in
his eyes and knew that Grandfather
Frog was feeling good-natured in spite
of his gruff greeting.

"If you please, Grandfather Frog, why
doesn't Mr. Greensnake wink at us when
we wink at him?" he asked.

"Chug-a-rum! Because he can't," replied Grandfather Frog.

"Can't!" cried Peter Rabbit and Johnny Chuck together.

"That's what I said — can't," replied Grandfather Frog. "And no more can Mr. Blacksnake, or Mr. Rattlesnake, or Mr. Gophersnake, or any other member of the Snake family."

"Why not?" cried Peter and Johnny, all in the same breath.

"Chug-a-rum!" said Grandfather Frog, folding his hands across his white and yellow waistcoat, "if you will sit still until I finish, I'll tell you; but if you move or ask any foolish questions, I'll stop right where I am, and you'll never hear the end of the story, for no one else knows it."

Of course Peter and Johnny promised to sit perfectly still and not say a word. After they had made themselves comfortable, Grandfather Frog cleared his throat as if to begin, but for a long time he didn't say a word. Once Peter opened his mouth to ask why, but remembered in time and closed it again without making a sound.

At last Grandfather Frog cleared his throat once more, and with a far-away look in his great, goggly eyes began:

"Once upon a time, long, long ago, when the world was young, lived old Mr. Snake, the grandfather a thousand times removed of little Mr. Greensnake and all the other Snakes whom you know. Of course he wasn't old then. He was young and spry and smart, was Mr. Snake. Now there is such a thing as being too smart. That was the trouble with Mr. Snake. Yes, Sir, that was the trouble with Mr. Snake. He was so smart that he soon found out that he was the smartest of all the

meadow and forest people, and that was
a bad thing. It certainly was a very
bad thing." Grandfather Frog shook his
head gravely.

"You see," he continued, "as soon as
he found that out, he began to take
advantage of his neighbors and cheat
them, but he would do it so smoothly
that they never once suspected that they
were being cheated. Mr. Snake would
go about all day cheating everybody he
met. At night he would go home and
chuckle over his smartness. It wasn't
long before he began to look down on his
neighbors for being so honest that they
didn't suspect other people of being
dishonest, and for being so easily
cheated.

"Now one bad habit almost always
leads to another. From cheating, Mr.
Snake just naturally slipped to stealing.
Yes, Sir, he became a thief. Of course

that made trouble right away, but still no one suspected Mr. Snake. He was always very polite to every one and always offering to do favors for his neighbors. In fact, Mr. Snake was very well liked and much respected. When any one had been robbed, he was always the first to offer sympathy and join in the hunt for the thief. He was so spry and slim, and could slip through the tall grass so fast, that he could go almost where he pleased without being seen, and this made him very bold. If he did happen to be found near the scene of trouble, he always had a story ready to account for his presence, and it sounded so true, and he told it in such an honest manner, that no one thought of doubting it.

"So Mr. Snake found that lying helped him to cheat and steal, and all the time he kept thinking how smart he was. But even Mr. Snake had a little bit of conscience, and once in a while it would trouble him. So what do you think he did? Why, cheating had become such a habit with him that he actually tried to cheat himself — to cheat his conscience! When he was telling a lie, he would wink one eye. 'That,' said he to himself, 'means that it isn't true, and if these folks are not smart enough to see me wink and know what it means, it is their own fault if they believe what I am telling them.' But always he took care to wink the eye that was turned away from the one he was talking to.

"Dear me, dear me, such terrible times as there were on the Green Meadows and in the Green Forest! They grew worse and worse, and when at last Old Mother Nature came to see how all the little people were getting along, she heard so many complaints

that she hardly knew where to begin to
straighten matters out. She had all the
little people come before her in turn and
tell their troubles. When it came Mr.
Snake's turn, he had no complaint to
make. He seemed to be the only one
who had no troubles. She asked him a
great many questions, and for each one
he had a ready reply. Of course a great
many of these replies were lies, and
every time he told one of these, he winked
without knowing it. You see, it had
become a habit.

"Now, with all his smartness, Mr.
Snake had forgotten one thing, one very
important thing. It was this: You can't
fool Old Mother Nature, and it is of no
use to try. He hadn't been talking
three minutes before she knew who was
at the bottom of all the trouble. She
let him finish, then called all the others
about her and told them who had made

all the trouble. Mr. Snake was very bold. He held his head very high in the air and pretended not to care. When Old Mother Nature turned her head, he even ran out his tongue at her, just as all the Snake family do at you and me to-day. When she had finished telling them how cheating and stealing and lying isn't smart at all, but very, very dreadful, she turned to Mr. Snake and said:

" 'From this time on, no one will believe anything you say, and you shall have no friends. You will never wink again, for you and your children and your children's children forever will have no eyelids, that all the world may know that those who make a wrong use of the things given them shall have them taken away.'

"And now you know why little Mr. Greensnake cannot wink at you; he hasn't any eyelids to wink with," finished Grandfather Frog.

Peter Rabbit drew a long breath. "Thank you, oh, thank you ever so much, Grandfather Frog," he said. "Will you tell us next time why Bobby Coon wears rings on his tail?"

"Perhaps," replied Grandfather Frog.

XI

WHY BOBBY COON HAS RINGS ON HIS TAIL

XI

WHY BOBBY COON HAS RINGS ON HIS TAIL

PETER RABBIT would give Grandfather Frog no peace. Every day Peter visited the Smiling Pool to tease Grandfather Frog for a story — for one particular story. He wanted to know why it is that Bobby Coon wears rings on his tail. You see, Peter had admired Bobby Coon's tail for a long time. Peter has such a funny little tail himself, just a little white bunch of cotton, that such a handsome tail as Bobby Coon's sometimes stirs just a wee bit of envy in Peter's heart.

But it wasn't envy so much as curiosity that prompted Peter to tease for that story. Bobby Coon's tail is very handsome, you know. It has beautiful rings of black and gray, and Peter didn't know of any other tail at all like it. Somehow, he felt right down deep in his heart that there must be a reason for those rings, just as there is a reason for his own long ears and long legs. The more he thought about it, the more he felt that he simply must know, and the only way he could find out was from Grandfather Frog, who is very old and very wise. So he teased and he teased until finally Grandfather Frog promised him that on the next afternoon he would tell Peter why Bobby Coon has rings on his tail. Peter hurried away to tell all the little meadow and forest people, and the next afternoon they were all on hand on the bank of the Smiling Pool to hear the story about Bobby Coon's tail.

"Chug-a-rum!" began Grandfather

Frog, smoothing down his white and yellow waistcoat. "Chug-a-rum! Some folks seem to think that what they do doesn't matter to anybody but themselves. That was the way with old Mr. Rabbit, who lived a long time ago when the world was young. He thought he could make all the trouble he pleased by his dreadful curiosity, and if he was found out, no one would suffer but himself. But it wasn't so. Here is Peter Rabbit, his grandchild a thousand times removed, with long legs and long ears, and the bad habit of curiosity, all because old Mr. Rabbit had a bad habit and didn't try to overcome it.

"It was the same way with old Mr. Coon. He was dishonest and stole from Old King Bear. Old Mother Nature punished him by putting mustard in his food, and Mr. Coon thought he was so smart that he could get ahead of Old

Mother Nature by washing all his food before he ate it. Old Mother Nature didn't say anything, but watched him and smiled to herself. You see, she knew that Mr. Coon was beginning a good habit, a very good habit indeed — the habit of neatness. So, though she knew perfectly well that he was doing it just to get ahead of her, she was glad, for she was fond of Mr. Coon in spite of the bad ways he had grown into, and she knew that good habits are like bad habits — once started they grow and grow, and are very likely to lead to more good habits.

"It was so with Mr. Coon. He found that his food tasted better for being so clean, and he grew very fussy about what he ate. No matter where he found it or how tempting it looked, he wouldn't eat it until he had carried it to the nearest water and washed it. He still remembered the mustard and tried to fool himself into thinking that he was simply spiting Old Mother Nature, but right down in his heart he knew that even if he should be told that never again would there be mustard in his food, he would wash it just the same.

"One day, as he sat beside the Laughing Brook eating his supper, he noticed that while his food had been washed clean, his hands were dirty. They spoiled his supper. Yes, Sir, they spoiled his supper.

"'What good does it do to wash my food, if I eat it out of dirty hands?' said Mr. Coon to himself, and he hurried to a quiet little pool to give them a good scrubbing. Then he washed his face and brushed his coat. 'Now I feel better, and I know my supper will taste better,' said he.

"From that time he began to be particular, very particular, about keeping himself clean, until finally there was no one on the Green Meadows or in the Green Forest quite so neat as Mr. Coon.

"Now at this time Mr. Coon had a very plain tail. It was all of one color, a grayish white, not at all pretty. Mr. Coon used to think a great deal about that tail and wish and wish that it was handsome. Sometimes he used to envy Mr. Fox his beautiful red tail with its black and white tip. One day, as he sat on an old log with his chin in his hands, thinking about his tail, who should come along but Old Mother Nature.

"'Good morning, Mr. Coon,' said she in her pleasantest voice.

"Mr. Coon got up and made a very low bow. 'Good morning, Mother Nature,' he replied in his politest manner, which was very polite indeed.

" 'What were you thinking about so hard?' asked Old Mother Nature.

"Mr. Coon looked a little bit ashamed. Then he sighed. 'I was wishing that my tail was handsomer,' said he. 'But it is a very good tail as it is,' he added hastily.

"Old Mother Nature's eyes twinkled. She sat down beside Mr. Coon and asked him all about his affairs, just as if she didn't know all about them already. She told him how pleased she was to find him so neat and clean, and Mr. Coon just tingled all over with pleasure. At last she got up to go, and her eyes twinkled more than ever, as she said:

" 'By the way, Mr. Coon, I am so pleased with your neatness that I am leaving you a reward. I hope you will like it.'

"Mr. Coon didn't see any reward, but he thanked her just the same, and Old Mother Nature went on her way. Mr.

Coon watched her out of sight. Then he sat down on the old log again and scratched his head thoughtfully as he looked this way and that.

" 'I wonder what she meant by reward. I don't see any anywhere,' he said to himself.

"By and by he just happened to glance at his tail. 'Oh!' cried Mr. Coon, and then for a long time he couldn't say another word, but just looked and looked with shining eyes and such a queer feeling of happiness in his heart. You see, Old Mother Nature had left a beautiful, broad, black ring around his tail. Mr. Coon couldn't do anything the rest of that day but look at and admire that ring, until his neck ached from twisting it around so long.

"After that he was neater than ever, you may be sure, and the next time Old Mother Nature came around, she left another handsome black ring on his tail, because he hadn't grown careless, but had kept up his good habits.

"Now about this time, hard times came to all the little people of the Green Forest and the Green Meadows. Every one began to grumble. Mr. Bear grumbled. Mr. Fox grumbled. Mr. Rabbit grumbled. Mr. Jay grumbled. Mr. Squirrel grumbled. Even Mr. Chuck grumbled. And one and all they began to blame Old Mother Nature. Then they began to quarrel among themselves and to steal from each other. Some even left their homes and went out into the Great World to try to find a better place to live, only to find that the Great World was a harder place to live in than the Green Forest and the Green Meadows.

"But Mr. Coon didn't grumble, and he didn't go away. No, Sir, Mr. Coon just stuck to his home and did the best he could to find enough to eat. He kept himself as neat as ever and was always cheerful. Whenever he met one of his grumbling neighbors, he would say:

" 'Better times coming! Better times coming! Old Mother Nature is doing the best she can. Better times coming!'

"The others would laugh at him for his faith in Old Mother Nature, and say ugly things about her, and urge Mr. Coon to go with them out into the Great World. But he kept right on minding his own business and keeping neat and cheerful, until at last Old Mother Nature, all worried and troubled, came to see what she could do to straighten matters out. It didn't take her long to find out how all the little meadow and forest people, except Mr. Coon, had grumbled and been discontented and said ugly things about her, for you can't fool Old Mother Nature, and it's of no use to try.

Some she punished one way, and some she punished another way, for of course she hadn't been to blame for the hard times, but had been working night and day to put an end to them.

"Mr. Coon was the last to be called before her, and instead of being frowning and cross, as she had been to the others, she was all smiles. She said a lot of nice things to him, and when at last she sent him away, what do you think she had given him?"

"More rings," cried Peter Rabbit.

"Yes," replied Grandfather Frog, "Mr. Coon's tail was ringed way to the tip. There was one for cheerfulness, and one for faith, and one for persistence in making the best of a bad matter and staying at home. And ever since that long-ago day when the world was young, the Coons have been very proud of their beautiful tails and have kept up the

good habits of old Mr. Coon. Now you
know, Peter Rabbit, why Bobby Coon
wears rings on his tail," concluded Grandfather Frog.

Peter gave a long sigh. "I think it's
perfectly beautiful," he said. "I wish
I had rings on my tail."

And then he wondered why everybody
laughed.

XII

WHY THERE IS A BLACK HEAD IN THE BUZZARD FAMILY

XII

WHY THERE IS A BLACK HEAD IN THE BUZZARD FAMILY

OL' MISTAH BUZZARD had just told the story of why he has a bald head and is proud of it. You know he hasn't a feather on it, and it is very, very red. It was a very interesting story, and it had been listened to with the closest attention by a lot of the little meadow and forest people. Unc' Billy Possum, who is Ol' Mistah Buzzard's particular friend, both having come from "way down souf," happened along just in time to hear the end of it.

"May Ah ask yo' a question, Brer Buzzard?" said he.

"Cert'nly, Brer Possum. Cert'nly," replied Ol' Mistah Buzzard.

"Is Buzzard really your fam'ly name?" asked Unc' Billy.

"No, Brer Possum, it isn't," replied Ol' Mistah Buzzard. Everybody looked surprised. You see, no one ever had heard him called anything but Buzzard. But no one said anything, and after a minute or two Ol' Mistah Buzzard explained.

"Mah fam'ly name is Vulture," said he. "Yes, Sah, mah fam'ly name is Vulture, but we-uns done been called Buzzards so long, that Ah don' know as Ah would know Ah was being spoken to, if Ah was called Mistah Vulture."

"An' do Ah understand that all of your fam'ly have red haids?" inquired Unc' Billy.

Ol' Mistah Buzzard looked down at Unc' Billy, and he saw a twinkle in Unc' Billy's shrewd little eyes. Ol' Mistah Buzzard grinned.

"Ah knows jes' what yo' done got in your mind, Brer Possum," said he. "It's that trifling, no 'count cousin of mine. He's a Buzzard, or a Vulture, if yo' like that better, jes' like Ah am, but he belongs to another branch of the fam'ly. He has a bald haid, jes' like Ah have, but his haid is black instead of red. That's because his grandpap was trifling an' po' trash, jes' like he is."

Peter Rabbit pricked up his ears. This sounded like another story. He was curious about that black-headed cousin of Ol' Mistah Buzzard, very curious indeed. He wondered if Ol' Mistah Buzzard would have to be teased for a story, like Grandfather Frog. Anyway, he would find out. There would be no harm in trying.

"If you please, how does your cousin happen to have a black head?" asked Peter as politely as he knew how.

"Because his grandpap asked too many questions," replied Ol' Mistah Buzzard, slyly winking at the others.

Everybody laughed, for everybody knows that no one asks more questions than Peter Rabbit. Peter laughed with the rest, although he looked a wee bit foolish. But he didn't mean to give up just because he was laughed at. Oh, my, no!

"Please, Mr. Buzzard, please tell us the story," he begged.

Now Ol' Mistah Buzzard is naturally good-natured and accommodating, and when Peter begged so hard, he just couldn't find it in his heart to refuse. Besides, he rather enjoys telling stories. So he shook his feathers out, half spread his wings to let the air blow under them, looked down at all the little meadow and forest people gathered about the foot of the tall, dead tree where he delights to roost, grinned at them in the funniest way, and then began this story:

"Way back in the days when Grandpap Buzzard had his lil falling out with ol' King Eagle and done fly so high he sco'tch the feathers offen his haid, he had a cousin, did Grandpap Buzzard, and this cousin was jes' naturally lazy and no 'count. Like most no 'count people, he used to make a regular nuisance of hisself, poking his nose into ev'ybody's business and never 'tending to his own. Wasn't anything going on that this trifling member of the Buzzard fam'ly didn't find out about and meddle in. He could ask mo' questions than Peter Rabbit can, an' anybody that can do that has got to ask a lot."

Everybody looked at Peter and laughed. Peter made a funny face and laughed too.

"Seemed like he jes' went 'round from

mo'ning to night asking questions," continued Ol' Mistah Buzzard. "Got so that eve'ybody dreaded to see that no 'count Buzzard coming, because he bound to pester with questions about things what don't concern him no ways.

"Now yo' know that way down in Ol' Virginny where Ah done come from, mah fam'ly done got the habit of sitting on the tops of chimneys in the wintertime to warm their toes."

"Why, I thought it was warm down south!" interrupted Peter Rabbit.

"So it is, Brer Rabbit! So it is!" Ol' Mistah Buzzard hastened to say. "But yo' see, ol' Jack Frost try to come down there sometimes, an' he cool the air off a right smart lot before he turn tail an' run back where he belong. So we-uns sit on the chimney-tops whenever ol' Jack Frost gets to straying down where he have no business. Yo' see, if we-uns keep our toes warm, we-uns are warm all over.

"One day this no 'count, trifling cousin of Grandpap Buzzard get cold in his feet. He look 'round right smart fo' a chimney fo' to warm his toes, an' pretty soon he see one where he never been before. It was on a lil ol' house, a lil ol' tumble-down house. Mistah Buzzard fly right over an' sit on that chimney-top fo' to warm his toes. Of course he right smart curious about that lil ol' tumble-down house and who live there. He hear somebody inside talking to theirself, but he can't hear what they say, jes' a mumbling sound that come up the chimney to him.

"He listen an' listen. Then he shift 'round to the other side of the chimney an' listen. No matter where he sit, he can't hear what being said down inside that lil ol' tumble-down house. Then what do yo' think Mistah Buzzard do? Why, he jes' stretch his fool haid as far down that chimney as he can an' listen an' listen. Yes, Sah, that is jes' what that no 'count Buzzard do. But all he hear is jes' a mumbling and a mumbling, an' that make him more curious than ever. It seem to him that he must go clean outen his haid 'less he hear what going on down inside that lil ol' house.

"Now when he stretch his haid an' neck down the chimney that way, he get 'em all black with soot. But he don't mind that. No, Sah, he don' mind that a bit. Fact is, he don' notice it. He so curious he don' notice anything, an' pretty soon he plumb fo'get where he is an' that he is listening where he have no business. He plumb fo'get all about this, an' he holler down that chimney. Yes, Sah, he holler right down that chimney!

" 'Will yo'-alls please speak a lil louder,' he holler down the chimney, jes' like that.

"Now the lil ol' woman what lived by herself in that lil ol' tumble-down house hadn't seen that no 'count Buzzard light on the chimney fo' to warm his toes, an' when she hear that voice coming right outen the fireplace, she was some flustrated and scared, was that lil ol' woman. Yes, Sah, she sho'ly was plumb scared. She so scared she tip over a whole kettleful of soup right in the fire. Of course that make a terrible mess an' a powerful lot of smoke an' hot ashes fly up the chimney. They like to choke that no 'count Buzzard to death. They burn the feathers offen his haid an' neck, an' the soot make him black, all but his feet an' laigs an' the inside of his wings, which he keep closed.

"Mistah Buzzard he give a mighty

squawk an' fly away. When he get home, he try an' try to brush that soot off, but it done get into the skin an' it stay there. An' from that day his haid an' neck stay black, an' he never speak lessen he spoken to, an' then he only grunt. His chillen jes' like him, an' his chillen's chillen the same way. An' that is the reason that mah cousin who lives down souf done have a black haid," concluded Ol' Mistah Buzzard.

A little sigh of satisfaction went around the circle of listeners. As usual, Peter Rabbit was the first to speak.

"That was a splendid story, Mr. Buzzard," said he, "and I'm ever and ever so much obliged to you. It was just as good as one of Grandfather Frog's."

Ol' Mistah Buzzard grinned and slowly winked one eye at Unc' Billy Possum as he replied: "Thank yo', Brer Rabbit.

That's quite the nicest thing yo' could say."

"But it's true!" shouted all together, and then everybody gave three cheers for Ol' Mistah Buzzard before starting off to attend to their own private affairs.

XIII

WHY BUSTER BEAR APPEARS TO HAVE NO TAIL

XIII

PETER RABBIT had something new
to bother his bump of curiosity.
And it did bother it a lot. He
had just seen Buster Bear for the first
time, and what do you think had im-
pressed him most? Well, it wasn't Buster's great size, or wonderful strength, or
big claws, or deep, grumbly-rumbly voice.
No, Sir, it wasn't one of these. It was
the fact that Buster Bear seemed to
have no tail! Peter couldn't get over
that. He almost pitied Buster Bear.
You see, Peter has a great admiration
for fine tails. He has always been rather
ashamed of the funny little one he has

himself. Still, it is a real tail, and he has often comforted himself with that thought.

So the first thing Peter did when he saw Buster Bear was to look to see what kind of a tail he had. Just imagine how surprised he was when he couldn't make sure that Buster had any tail at all. There was something that might, just might, be meant for a tail, and Peter wasn't even sure of that. If it was, it was so ridiculously small that Peter felt that he had no reason to be ashamed of his own tail.

He was still thinking about this when he started for home. Half way there, he paused, saw that the way to the Smiling Pool was clear, and suddenly made up his mind to ask Grandfather Frog about Buster Bear's tail. Off he started, lipperty-lipperty-lip.

"Oh, Grandfather Frog," he panted,

as soon as he reached the edge of the Smiling Pool, "has Buster Bear got a tail?"

Grandfather Frog regarded Peter in silence for a minute or two.

Then very slowly he asked: "What are your eyes for, Peter Rabbit? Couldn't you see whether or not he has a tail?"

"No, Grandfather Frog, I really couldn't tell whether he has a tail or not," replied Peter quite truthfully. "At first I thought he hadn't, and then I thought he might have. If he has, it doesn't seem to me that it is enough to call a really truly tail."

"Well, it is a really truly tail, even if you don't think so," retorted Grandfather Frog, "and he has it for a reminder."

"A reminder!" exclaimed Peter, looking very much puzzled. "A reminder of what?"

Grandfather Frog cleared his throat two or three times. "Sit down, Peter, and learn a lesson from the tale of the tail of Old King Bear," said he very seriously.

"You remember that once upon a time, long ago, when the world was young, Old King Bear ruled in the Green Forest, and everybody brought tribute to him."

Peter nodded and Grandfather Frog went on.

"Now Old King Bear was the great-great-ever-so-great grandfather of Buster Bear, and he looked very much as Buster does, except that he didn't have any tail at all, not the least sign of a tail. At first, before he was made king of the Green Forest, he didn't mind this at all. In fact, he was rather pleased that he didn't have a tail. You see, he couldn't think of any earthly use he would have

for a tail, and so he was glad that he
hadn't got one to bother with.

"This was just Old Mother Nature's
view of the matter.   She had done her
very best to give everybody everything
that they really needed, and not to give
them things which they didn't need.
She couldn't see that Mr. Bear had the
least need of a tail, and so she hadn't
given him one.   Mr. Bear was perfectly
happy without one, and was so busy
getting enough to eat that he didn't have
time for silly thoughts or vain wishes.

"Then he was made king over all the
people of the Green Forest, and his word
was law.   It was a very great honor,
and for a while he felt it so and did his
best to rule wisely.   He went about just
as before, hunting for his living, and had
no more time than before for foolish
thoughts or vain wishes.   But after a
little, the little people over whom he

ruled began to bring him tribute, so that he no longer had to hunt for enough to eat. Indeed, he had so much brought to him, that he couldn't begin to eat all of it, and he grew very dainty and fussy about what he did eat. Having nothing to do but eat and sleep, he grew very fat and lazy, as is the case with most people who have nothing to do. He grew so fat that when he walked, he puffed and wheezed. He grew so lazy that he wanted to be waited on all the time.

"It happened about this time that he overheard Mr. Fox talking to Mr. Wolf when they both thought him asleep. 'A pretty kind of a king, he is!' sneered Mr. Fox. 'The idea of a king without a tail!'

"'That's so,' assented Mr. Wolf. 'Why, even that little upstart, Mr. Rabbit, has got a make-believe tail.'"

Grandfather Frog's eyes twinkled as

he said this, and Peter looked very much embarrassed. But he didn't say anything, so Grandfather Frog went on.

"Old King Bear pretended to wake up just then, and right away Mr. Fox and Mr. Wolf were as polite and smiling as you please and began to flatter him. They told him how proud they were of their king, and how handsome he was, and a lot of other nice things, all of which he had heard often before and had believed. He pretended to believe them now, but after they were through paying their respects and had gone away, he kept turning over and over in his mind what he had overheard them say when they thought he was asleep.

"After that he couldn't think of anything but the fact that he hadn't any tail. He took particular notice of all who came to pay him tribute, and he saw that every one of them had a tail.

Some had long tails; some had short tails; some had handsome tails and some had homely tails; but everybody had a tail of some kind. The more he tried not to think of these tails, the more he did think of them. The more he thought of them, the more discontented he grew because he had none. He didn't stop to think that probably all of them had use for their tails. No, Sir, he didn't think of that. Everybody else had a tail, and he hadn't. He felt that it was a disgrace that he, the king, should have no tail. He brooded over it so much that he lost his appetite and grew cross and peevish.

"Then along came Old Mother Nature to see how things were going in the Green Forest. Of course she saw right away that something was wrong with Old King Bear. When she asked him what the matter was, he was ashamed to tell her at first. But after a little he told her that he wanted a tail; that he could never again be happy unless he had a tail. She told him that he hadn't the least use in the world for a tail, and that he wouldn't be any happier if he had one. Nothing that she could say made any difference — he wanted a tail. Finally she gave him one.

"For a few days Old King Bear was perfectly happy. He spent all his spare time admiring his new tail. He called the attention of all his subjects to it, and they all told him that it was a very wonderful tail and was very becoming to him. But it wasn't long before he found that his new tail was very much in the way. It bothered him when he walked. It was in the way when he sat down. It was a nuisance when he climbed a tree. He didn't have a single use for it, and yet he had to carry it with him wherever he went. Worse still, he overheard little

Mr. Squirrel and Mr. Possum making fun of it. And then he discovered that the very ones who admired his tail so to his face were laughing at him and poking fun at him behind his back.

"And then Old King Bear wished that he *hadn't* a tail more than ever he wished that he *did* have a tail. Again he lost his appetite and grew cross and peevish, so that no one dared come near him. So matters went from bad to worse, until once more Old Mother Nature visited the Green Forest to see how things were. Very humbly Old King Bear went down on his knees and begged her to take away his tail. At first Old Mother Nature refused, but he begged so hard and promised so faithfully never again to be discontented, that finally she relented and took away his tail, all but just a wee little bit. That she left as a reminder lest he should forget the lesson

"Then Old King Bear wished that he hadn't a tail."

he had learned and should again grow envious.

"And every bear since that long-ago day has carried about with him a reminder — you can hardly call it a real tail — of the silly, foolish discontent of Old King Bear," concluded Grandfather Frog.

Peter Rabbit scratched one long ear thoughtfully as he replied: "Thank you, Grandfather Frog. I think that hereafter I will be quite content with what I've got and never want things it is not meant that I should have."

XIV

WHY FLITTER THE BAT FLIES AT NIGHT

XIV

FLITTER the Bat made Peter Rabbit's head dizzy. Peter couldn't help watching him. He just had to. It seemed so wonderful that Flitter could really fly, that whenever he saw him, Peter had to stop and watch. And then, as he saw Flitter twist and turn, fly high, fly low, and go round and round, Peter's head would begin to swim and grow dizzy, and he wondered and wondered how it was that Flitter himself didn't grow dizzy.

"It must be fine to fly," thought Peter. "I wish I could fly. If I could, I wouldn't spend all my time flying around the way

Flitter does. I'd go on long journeys and see the Great World. I'd fly way, way up in the blue, blue sky, the way Ol' Mistah Buzzard does, where I could look down and see all that is going on in the Green Forest and on the Green Meadows. And I'd fly in the daytime, because there is more going on then. I wonder, now, why it is that Flitter never comes out until after jolly, round, red Mr. Sun has gone to bed behind the Purple Hills. I never see him in the daytime, and I don't even know where he keeps himself. I never thought of it before, but I wonder why it is that he flies only at night. I believe I'll ask Grandfather Frog the very next time I see him."

Now you know that once Peter Rabbit's curiosity is aroused, it just has to be satisfied. No sooner did he begin to wonder about Flitter the Bat than he could think of nothing else. So he watched until the way was clear, and then he started for the Smiling Pool as fast as he could go, lipperty-lipperty-lip. He hoped he would find Grandfather Frog sitting as usual on his big green lily-pad, and that he would be good-natured. If he wasn't feeling good-natured, it would be of no use to ask him for a story.

When Peter reached the Smiling Pool he was disappointed, terribly disappointed. The big green lily-pad was there, but there was no one sitting on it. Somehow the Smiling Pool didn't seem quite like itself without Grandfather Frog sitting there watching for foolish green flies. Peter's face showed just how disappointed he felt. He was just going to turn away when a great, deep voice said:

"Chug-a-rum! Where are your manners, Peter Rabbit, that you forget to speak to your elders?"

Peter stared eagerly into the Smiling Pool, and presently he saw two great, goggly eyes and the top of a green head, way out almost in the middle of the Smiling Pool. It was Grandfather Frog himself, having his morning swim.

"Oh, Grandfather Frog, I didn't see you at all!" cried Peter. "If I had, of course I would have spoken. The fact is, I — I ——"

"You want a story," finished Grandfather Frog for him. "You can't fool me, Peter Rabbit. You came over here just to ask me for a story. I know you, Peter! I know you! Well, what is it this time?"

"If you please," replied Peter politely and happily, for he saw that Grandfather Frog was feeling good-natured, "why is it that Flitter the Bat flies only at night?"

Grandfather Frog climbed out on his big green lily-pad and made himself comfortable. Peter sat still and tried not to show how impatient he felt. Grandfather Frog took his time. It tickled him to see how hard impatient Peter was trying to be patient, and his big, goggly eyes twinkled.

"Chug-a-rum!" said he at last, with a suddenness that made Peter jump. "That's very good, Peter, very good indeed! Now I'll tell you the story."

Of course he meant that Peter's effort to keep still was very good, but Peter didn't know this, and he couldn't imagine what Grandfather Frog meant. However, what he cared most about was the story, so he settled himself to listen, his long ears standing straight up, and his eyes stretched wide open as he watched

Grandfather Frog. The latter cleared his throat two or three times, each time as if he intended to begin right then. It was one of Grandfather Frog's little jokes. He did it just to tease Peter. At last he really did begin, and the very first thing he did was to ask Peter a question.

"What is the reason that you stay in the dear Old Briar-patch when Reddy Fox is around?"

"So that he won't catch me, of course," replied Peter.

"Very good," said Grandfather Frog. "Now, why do you go over to the sweet-clover patch every day?"

"Why, because there is plenty to eat there," replied Peter, looking very, very much puzzled.

"Well, now you've answered your own question," grunted Grandfather Frog. "Flitter flies at night because he is safest then, and because he can find plenty to eat."

"Oh," said Peter, and his voice sounded dreadfully disappointed. He had found out what he had wanted to know, but he hadn't had a story. He fidgeted about and looked very hard at Grandfather Frog, but the latter seemed to think that he had told Peter what he wanted to know, and that was all there was to it. Finally Peter sighed, and it was such a heavy sigh! Then very slowly he turned his back on the Smiling Pool and started to hop away.

"Chug-a-rum!" said Grandfather Frog in his deepest, story-telling voice. "A long time ago when the world was young, the great-great-ever-so-great grandfather of Flitter the Bat first learned to fly."

"I know!" cried Peter eagerly. "You told me about that, and it was a splendid story."

"But when he learned to fly, he found that Old Mother Nature never gives all her blessings to any single one of her little people," continued Grandfather Frog, without paying the least attention to Peter's interruption. "Old Mr. Bat had wings, something no other animal had, but he found that he could no longer run and jump. He could just flop about on the ground, and was almost helpless. Of course that meant that he could very easily be caught, and so the ground was no longer a safe place for him. But he soon found that he was not safe in the air in daytime. Old Mr. Hawk could fly even faster than he, and Mr. Hawk was always watching for him. At first, Mr. Bat didn't know what to do. He didn't like to go to Old Mother Nature and complain that his new wings were not all that he had thought they would be. That would look as if he were ungrateful for her kindness in giving him the wings.

" 'I've got to think of some way out of my troubles myself,' thought old Mr. Bat. 'When I'm sure that I can't, it will be time enough to go to Old Mother Nature.'

"Now of course it is very hard to think when you are twisting and dodging and turning in the air."

"Of course!" said Peter Rabbit, just as if he knew all about it.

"So Mr. Bat went looking for a place where he could be quiet all by himself and think without danger of being gobbled up for some one's dinner," continued Grandfather Frog. "He flew and he flew and had almost given up hope of finding any such place when he saw a cave. It looked very black inside, but it was big enough for Mr. Bat to fly into, and in he went. He knew that

Mr. Hawk would never come in there, and when he found a little shelf up near the roof, he knew that he was safe from any four-footed enemies who might follow him there. It was just the place to rest and think. So he rested, and while he rested, he thought and thought.

"By and by he noticed that it was growing dark outside. ' My goodness! If I am going to get anything to eat to-day, I shall have to hurry,' thought he. When he got outside, he found that Mr. Sun had gone to bed. So had all the birds, except Mr. Owl and Mr. Nighthawk. Now Mr. Nighthawk doesn't belong to the Hawk family at all, so there was nothing to fear from him. Then Mr. Bat had a very pleasant surprise. He found the air full of insects, ever so many more than in the daytime. By being very smart and quick he caught a few before it was too dark for him to see. They didn't fill his stomach, but they kept him from starving. As he flew back to the cave, a great idea came to him, the idea for which he had been thinking so hard. He would sleep days in the cave, where he was perfectly safe, and come out to hunt bugs and insects just as soon as Mr. Hawk had gone to bed! Then he would be safe and would not have to complain to Old Mother Nature.

"At first old Mr. Bat, who wasn't old then, you know, had hard work to catch enough insects before it grew too dark, but he found that every night he could see a little longer and a little better than the night before, until by and by he could see as well in the dusk as he used to see in the daytime. Then he realized that Old Mother Nature had once more been very good to him, and that she had helped him just as she always helps those who help themselves. She had given him night-seeing eyes, and he no more had to go hungry.

"Mr. Bat was very grateful, and from that day to this, Bats have been content to live in caves and fly in the evening. You ask Flitter if it isn't so."

Peter grinned. "He never stays in one place long enough for me to ask him anything," said he. "I'm ever so much obliged for the story, Grandfather Frog. It pays to make the best of what we have, doesn't it?"

"It certainly does. Chug-a-rum! It certainly does!" replied Grandfather Frog.

XV

WHY SPOTTY THE TURTLE CARRIES HIS HOUSE WITH HIM

XV

WHY SPOTTY THE TURTLE CARRIES HIS HOUSE WITH HIM

SPOTTY the Turtle sat on an old log on the bank of the Smiling Pool, taking a sun-bath. He had sat that way for the longest time without once moving. Peter Rabbit had seen him when he went by on his way to the Laughing Brook and the Green Forest to look for some one to pass the time of day with. Spotty was still there when Peter returned a long time after, and he didn't look as if he had moved. A sudden thought struck Peter. He couldn't remember that he ever had seen Spotty's house. He had seen the houses of most of his other friends, but think as hard as ever he could, he didn't remember having seen Spotty's.

"Hi, Spotty!" he shouted. "Where do you live?"

Spotty slowly turned his head and looked up at Peter. There was a twinkle in his eyes, though Peter didn't see it.

"Right here in the Smiling Pool. Where else should I live?" he replied.

"I mean, where is your house?" returned Peter. "Of course I know you live in the Smiling Pool, but where is your house? Is it in the bank or down under water?"

"It is just wherever I happen to be. Just now it is right here," said Spotty. "I always take it with me wherever I go; I find it much the handiest way."

With that Spotty disappeared. That is to say, his head and legs and tail disappeared. Peter stared very hard. Then he began to laugh, for it came to him that what Spotty had said was true. His house was with him, and now he had simply retired inside. He didn't need any other house than just that hard, spotted shell, inside of which he was now so cosily tucked away.

"That's a great idea! Ho, ho, ho! That's a great idea!" shouted Peter.

"Of course it is," replied Spotty, putting nothing but his head out. "You will always find me at home whenever you call, Peter, and that is more than you can say of most other people."

All the way to his own home in the dear Old Briar-patch, Peter thought about Spotty and how queer it was that he should carry his house around with him.

"I wonder how it happens that he does it," thought he. "No wonder he is so slow. Of course, it is very handy to have his house always with him. As he says, he is always at home. Still, when he is in a hurry to get away from an enemy, it must be very awkward to have to carry his house on his back. I — I — why, how stupid of me! He doesn't have to run away at all! All he has got to do is to go inside his house and stay there until the danger is past! I never thought of that before. Why, that is the handiest thing I ever heard of."

Now Peter knew that there must be a good story about Spotty and his house, and you know Peter dearly loves a good story. So at the very first opportunity the next day, he hurried over to the Smiling Pool to ask Grandfather Frog about it. As usual, Grandfather Frog was sitting on his big green lily-pad. No sooner did Peter pop his head above the edge of the bank of the Smiling Pool than Grandfather Frog exclaimed:

"Chug-a-rum! You've kept me waiting a long time, Peter Rabbit. I don't like to be kept waiting. If you wanted to know about Spotty the Turtle, why didn't you come earlier?" All the time there was a twinkle in the big, goggly eyes of Grandfather Frog.

Peter was so surprised that he couldn't find his tongue. He hadn't said a word to any one about Spotty, so how could Grandfather Frog know what he had come for? For a long time he had had a great deal of respect for Grandfather Frog, who, as you know, is very old and very wise, but now Peter felt almost afraid of him. You see, it seemed to Peter as if Grandfather Frog had read his very thoughts.

"I — I didn't know you were waiting. Truly I didn't," stammered Peter. "If I had, I would have been here long ago. If you please, how did you know that I was coming and what I was coming for?"

"Never mind how I knew. I know a great deal that I don't tell, which is more than some folks can say," replied Grandfather Frog.

Peter wondered if he meant him, for you know Peter is a great gossip. But he didn't say anything, because he didn't know just what to say, and in a minute Grandfather Frog began the story Peter so much wanted.

"Of course you know, without me telling you, that there is a reason for Spotty's carrying his house around with him, because there is a reason for everything in this world. And of course you know that that reason is because of something that happened a long time ago, way back in the days when the world was young. Almost everything to-day is the result of things that happened in those long-ago days. The great-great-ever-so-

great grandfather of Spotty the Turtle
lived then, and unlike Spotty, whom
you know, he had no house. He was
very quiet and bashful, was Mr. Turtle,
and he never meddled with any one's
business, because he believed that the
best way of keeping out of trouble was
to attend strictly to his own affairs.

"He was a good deal like Spotty, just
as fond of the water and just as slow
moving, but he didn't have the house
which Spotty has now. If he had had,
he would have been saved a great deal
of trouble and worry. For a long time
everybody lived at peace with everybody
else. Then came the trying time, of
which you already know, when those
who lived on the Green Meadows and
in the Green Forest had the very hardest
kind of work to find enough to eat, and
were hungry most of the time. Now
Mr. Turtle, living in the Smiling Pool,

had plenty to eat. He had nothing to worry about on that score. Everybody who lives in the Smiling Pool knows that it is the best place in the world, anyway."

Grandfather Frog winked at Jerry Muskrat, who was listening, and Jerry nodded his head.

"But presently Mr. Turtle discovered that the big people were eating the little people whenever they could catch them, and that he wasn't safe a minute when on shore, and not always safe in the water," continued Grandfather Frog. "He had two or three very narrow escapes, and these set him to thinking. He was too slow and awkward to run or to fight. The only thing he could do was to keep out of sight as much as possible. So he learned to swim with only his head out of water, and sometimes with only the end of his nose out of water. When he went on land, he would cover himself with mud, and then when he heard anybody coming, he would lie perfectly still, with his legs and his tail and his head drawn in just as close as possible, so that he looked for all the world like just a little lump of brown earth.

"One day he had crawled under a piece of bark to rest and at the same time keep out of sight of any who might happen along. When he got ready to go on his way, he found that the piece of bark had caught on his back, and that he was carrying it with him. At first he was annoyed and started to shake it off. Before he succeeded, he heard someone coming, so he promptly drew in his head and legs and tail. It was Mr. Fisher, and he was very hungry and fierce. He looked at the piece of bark under which Mr. Turtle was hiding, but all he saw was the bark, because, you

know, Mr. Turtle had drawn himself
wholly under.

"'I believe,' said Mr. Fisher, talking
out loud to himself, 'that I'll have a
look around the Smiling Pool and see if
I can catch that slow-moving Turtle
who lives there. I believe he'll make
me a good dinner.'

"Of course Mr. Turtle heard just what
he said, and he blessed the piece of bark
which had hidden him from Mr. Fisher's
sight. For a long time he lay very still.
When he did go on, he took the greatest
care not to shake off that piece of bark,
for he didn't know but that any minute
he might want to hide under it again.
At last he reached the Smiling Pool and
slipped into the water, leaving the piece
of bark on the bank. Thereafter, when
he wanted to go on land, he would first
make sure that no one was watching.
Then he would crawl under the piece of

bark and get it on his back. Wherever he went he carried the piece of bark so as to have it handy to hide under.

"Now all this time Old Mother Nature had been watching Mr. Turtle, and it pleased her to see that he was smart enough to think of such a clever way of fooling his enemies. So she began to study how she could help Mr. Turtle. One day she came up behind him just as he sat down to rest. The piece of bark was uncomfortable and scratched his back. 'I wish,' said he, talking to himself, for he didn't know that any one else was near, 'I wish that I had a house of my own that I could carry on my back all the time and be perfectly safe when I was inside of it.'

" 'You shall have,' said Old Mother Nature, and reaching out, she touched his back and turned the skin into hard shell. Then she touched the skin of his stomach and turned that into hard shell. 'Now draw in your head and your legs and your tail,' said she.

"Mr. Turtle did as he was told to do, and there he was in the very best and safest kind of a house, perfectly hidden from all his enemies!

"'Oh, Mother Nature, how can I ever thank you?' he cried.

"'By doing as you always have done, attending wholly to your own affairs,' replied Old Mother Nature.

"So ever since that long-ago day when the world was young, all Turtles have carried their houses with them and never have meddled in things that don't concern them," concluded Grandfather Frog.

"Oh, thank you, Grandfather Frog," exclaimed Peter, drawing a long breath. "That was a perfectly splendid thing for Old Mother Nature to do."

Then he started for his own home in

the dear Old Briar-patch, and all the way there he wondered and wondered how Grandfather Frog knew that he wanted that story, and to this day he hasn't found out. You see, he didn't notice that Grandfather Frog was listening when he asked Spotty about his house. Of course, Grandfather Frog knows Peter and his curiosity so well that he had guessed right away that Peter would come to him for the story, just as Peter did.

XVI

USUALLY the thing that interests us most is something that we haven't got ourselves. It is that way with Peter Rabbit. Peter is not naturally envious. Oh, my, no! Peter is pretty well satisfied with what he has, which is quite as it should be. There is only one thing with which Peter is really dissatisfied, and it is only once in a while, when he hasn't much of anything else to think about, that he is dissatisfied with this. Can you guess what it is? Well, it is his tail. Yes, Sir, that is the one thing that ever really troubles Peter.

You see, Peter's tail is nothing but a funny little bunch of cotton, which doesn't look like a tail at all. The only time he ever sees it is when he is back to the Smiling Pool and looks over his shoulder at his reflection in the water, and then, of course, he really doesn't see his tail itself. So sometimes when Peter sees the fine tails of his neighbors, a little bit of envy creeps into his heart for just a little while. Why, even little Danny Meadow Mouse has a real tail, short as it is. And as for Happy Jack Squirrel and Reddy Fox and Bobby Coon and Jimmy Skunk, everybody knows what beautiful tails they have. Once Peter thought about it so much that Grandfather Frog noticed how sober he was and asked Peter what the trouble was. When Peter told him that it seemed to him that Old Mother Nature had not been fair in giving him such a foolish little tail when she had given others such beautiful ones, Grandfather Frog just opened his big mouth and laughed until he had to hold his sides.

"Why, Peter," said he, "you look so sober, that I thought you really had something to worry about. What would you do with a big tail, if you had one? It would always be in your way. Just think how many times Reddy Fox or old Granny Fox have almost caught you. They certainly would have before this, if you had had a long tail sticking out behind for them to get hold of. I had a long tail when I was young, and I was mighty glad to get rid of it."

After he heard that, Peter felt better But he didn't lose interest in tails, and he spent a great deal of time in wondering why some of his neighbors had big, bushy tails and some had long, slim tail and why he himself had almost no tail at all. So when Paddy the Beaver came to live in the Green Forest, and made a pond there by building a wonderful dam across the Laughing Brook, the first thing Peter looked to see was what kind of a tail Paddy has, and the first time he got a good look at it, his eyes popped almost out of his head. He just stared and stared. He hardly noticed the wonderful dam or the equally wonderful canals which Paddy had made. All he could think of was that great, broad, flat, thick tail, which is so unlike any tail he had ever seen or heard of.

The very next morning he hurried over to the Smiling Pool to tell Grandfather Frog about it. Grandfather Frog's big, goggly eyes twinkled.

"Chug-a-rum!" said he. "Paddy the Beaver has one of the most useful tails I know of. Would you like to know now he comes by such a queer tail?"

The first thing Peter looked to see was what kind of
a tail Paddy has.

"Oh, if you please! If you please, Grandfather Frog! I didn't suppose there was such a queer tail in all the world, and I don't see what possible use it can be. Do tell me about it!" cried Peter.

"Chug-a-rum! If you had used your eyes when you visited Paddy, you might have guessed for yourself how he came by it," replied Grandfather Frog gruffly. "Some people never do learn to use their eyes."

Peter looked a bit sheepish, but he said nothing and waited patiently. Presently Grandfather Frog cleared his throat two or three times and began to talk.

"Once upon a time, long, long ago, when the world was young ——"

"It seems to me that everything wonderful happened long ago when the world was young," interrupted Peter.

Grandfather Frog looked at Peter severely, and Peter hastened to beg his pardon.

After a long time Grandfather Frog began again.

"Once on a time, long, long ago, lived Mr. Beaver, the great-great-ever-so-great grandfather of Paddy up there in the Green Forest. Old Mr. Beaver was one of the hardest working of all of Old Mother Nature's big family and one of the smartest, just as Paddy is to-day. He always seemed happiest when he was busiest, and because he liked to be happy all the time, he tried to keep busy all the time.

"He was very thrifty, was Mr. Beaver; not at all like some people I know. He believed in preparing to-day for what might happen to-morrow, and so when he had all the food he needed for the present, he stored away food for the time when it might not be so easy to get. And he believed in helping himself, did Mr. Beaver, and not in leaving everything to Old Mother Nature, as did most of his neighbors. That is how he first came to think of making a dam and a pond. Like his small cousin, Mr. Muskrat, he was very fond of the water, and felt most at home and safest there. But he found that sometimes the food which he liked best, which was the bark of certain kinds of trees, grew some distance from the water, and it was the hardest kind of hard work to roll and drag the logs down to the water, where he could eat the bark from them in safety.

"He thought about this a great deal, but instead of going to Old Mother Nature and complaining, as most of his neighbors would have done in his place, he studied and studied to find some way to make the work easier. One day he noticed that a lot of sticks had caught in the stream where he made his home, and that because the water could not work its way between them as fast as where nothing hindered it, it made a little pool just above the sticks. That made him think harder than ever. He brought some of the logs and sticks from which he had gnawed the bark and fastened them with the others, and right away the pool grew bigger. The more sticks he added, the bigger the pool grew. Mr. Beaver had discovered what a dam is for and how to build it.

"'Why,' thought he, 'if I make a pond at the place nearest to my food trees, I can carry the water to the trees instead of the trees to the water; and that will be easier and ever so much safer as well.'

"So Mr. Beaver built a dam at just the right place, while all the other little people laughed at him and made fun of him for working so hard. Just as he had thought it would do, the dam made a pond, and the pond grew bigger and bigger, until it reached the very place where his food trees grew. Mr. Beaver built him a big, comfortable house out in the pond, and then he went to work as hard as ever he could to cut down trees and then cut them up into the right sized pieces to store away in his big food pile for the winter.

"Now cutting down trees is hard work. Yes, Siree, cutting down trees is the hardest kind of hard work. Mr. Beaver had to sit up on his hind legs to do it, and his legs grew very, very tired. In those days he had a tail very much like the tail of Jerry Muskrat. It was very useful when he was swimming, but it was of no use at all at any other time. Some-times he tried to brace himself with it —

when he was sitting up to cut trees, and found it of no help. But he didn't complain; he just kept right on working, and only stopped to rest when his legs ached so that he had to.

"He was working just as usual one day when Old Mother Nature came along to see how he was getting on. She saw the new dam and the new pond, and she asked Mr. Beaver who had made them. He told her that he had and explained why. Old Mother Nature was greatly pleased, but she didn't say so. She just passed the time of day with him and then sat down to watch him cut a tree. She saw him try to brace himself with his useless tail, and she saw him stop to rest his tired legs.

" 'That looks to me like pretty hard work,' said Old Mother Nature.

" 'So it is,' replied Mr. Beaver, stretching first one leg and then another. 'But things worth having are worth working for,' and with that he began cutting again.

" 'You ought to have something to sit on,' said Old Mother Nature, her eyes twinkling.

"Mr. Beaver grinned. 'It would be very nice,' he confessed, 'but I never waste time wishing for things I haven't got and can't get,' and went right on cutting.

"The next morning when he awoke, he had the greatest surprise of his life. He had a new tail! It was broad and thick and flat. It wasn't like any tail he had ever seen or heard of. At first he didn't know how to manage it, but when he tried to swim, he found that it was even better than his old tail for swimming. He hurried over to begin his day's work, and there he made another discovery; his new tail was just the most splendid brace! It was almost like a stool to sit on, and he could work all day long without tiring his legs. Then was Mr. Beaver very happy, and to show how happy he was, he worked harder than ever. Later, he found that his new tail was just what he needed to pat down the mud with which he covered the roof of his house.

" 'Why,' he cried, 'I believe it is the most useful tail in all the world!'

"And then he wished with all his might that Old Mother Nature would return so that he might thank her for it. And that," concluded Grandfather Frog, "is how Mr. Beaver came by his broad tail. You see, Old Mother Nature always helps those who help themselves. And ever since that long-ago day, all Beavers have had broad tails, and have been the greatest workers in the world."